# Armageddon: The Final Agenda

**Pam Vause**

ISBN-13: 978-1-4796-1393-9 (Paperback)
ISBN-13: 978-1-4796-1394-6 (ePub)
Library of Congress Control Number: 2021904247

The website references in this book have been shortened using a URL shortener and redirect service called 1ref.us, which TEACH Services manages. If you find that a reference no longer works, please contact us and let us know which one is not working so that we can correct it. Any personal website addresses that the author included are managed by the author. TEACH Services is not responsible for the accuracy or permanency of any links.

Published by

# Contents

# Acknowledgements

I wish to thank:
My husband, for all his support while writing this book.
Pastor M. Brownhill and Doctor P. Harold for editing my work.

Pamela Vause

# Prologue

## *Modern Rome Twenty-first Century*

Father Frank Finke stood transfixed, staring at the pavement in front of him. A large circle of tiles depicted a wheel within a wheel. Protruding from the centre was a large obelisk. Behind all this, glistening in the sun, was the magnificent dome of St Peter's Basilica. He drew in his breath: he could hardly believe he was at the Vatican! His lifelong dream had come to fruition.

Father Frank was a Catholic priest from Neunkirchen village in the mountains of Austria. He had served and ministered in his parish for twenty years, and while conducting his round of duties, had studied to become a Jesuit priest. His initiation was to be held at the Vatican.

A priest stepped from the shadows of the pillared verandas. Father Frank walked toward him and introduced himself. "I'm Frank Finke from Austria." He pulled an official invitation from his pocket. "I have this invitation to attend the initiation ceremony tomorrow." He spoke to the priest in Italian here in Vatican City, but he could also speak five other languages, including English.

The priest nodded. "I'm here to direct you. Go to the end of this walkway, and on the right, you'll see a door. Go in there," he explained.

Father Frank entered an expansive corridor with stark walls. A man behind a desk offered him a pen to sign the register. "Please wait here for an attendant," he instructed. "He'll take you to your room."

A priest took him in a different direction from all the pomp and glory of the Vatican that millions of tourists visited each year. Instead, he took him to the humble priests' quarters, consisting of a two-room suite with a stone floor and minimal furnishings. Father Frank threw his small bag onto the bed. He ran his hand through his thin, grey hair and sighed deeply. His face was sombre as he remembered the days of his training.

The next morning, one hundred men gathered in the priests' great hall. Father Frank's face clouded; he didn't take kindly to large groups.

Here they were led to the Vatican's heart, where High Mass was held. All would receive their new postings to different countries from where they now lived. But most important was to take the Jesuit oath that was an important part of the initiation.

Father Frank sat in front of the magnificent serpentine columns that supported Bernini's canopy. In awe, he looked at magnificent paintings, statues, and carvings. Gold inlays and artwork were to be seen everywhere. Pope Nicholas entered and sat in front of the altar while the Vatican choir sang in sweet, pure harmony. They sang to the pope, *"You are our king, our Lord, and ruler."*

Amongst all this splendour, Pope Nicholas addressed his one hundred Jesuits. "I wish to encourage you, my children. You have been chosen for a special work, and you'll answer to no one but me. Your position is very important as it involves future events that will shape the New World Order. You will be part of the modern Jesuit society, working with the Vatican for world peace. You'll work with communities and other churches to bring mankind into unity, and under our banner," he informed them.

"One hundred nations have signed a peace treaty with our Vatican," he continued. "Our cardinals have been placed in all major countries in the ten world zones. They are to work as ambassadors within these different regions. Through this means we will infiltrate the entire world with our presence. We will have our people in churches, governments, and financial sectors throughout the world."

He paused for a moment, and a look of sheer cunning crossed his face. "You realise the largest shareholder in the World Bank is us, the Vatican. In the last recession to save the economy, the World Bank injected trillions of dollars into the United States and many other major countries. As you can see, through our support, we will once again rule the world."

Frank was amazed at how the papacy had the world depending on them. He smiled smugly. *Yes*, he thought, *it will make easy work for our secret society.*

* * *

Father Frank retired to his room. Late that evening, a tap was heard on his door. He had been ready for some time.

"It's time,"' said a gruff voice, and a lamp was thrust into his hands. Lamp-holding, dark figures passed by. They were twenty of the hundred newly-ordained priests, from all walks of life, but there for a different purpose and agenda.

Father Frank followed the head Jesuit, who led them through dark tunnels. As he walked, he locked his gaze on the cloaked figure in front of him, and his mind raced back to the original purpose of the Templar Order. They were the papacy knights who protected the walls of Jerusalem from invading Muslim armies. They were the Vatican's army. *I'm about to become one of them*, he thought. *Our secret order will destroy all dissenters of the New World Order.* With fear and apprehension, he stole a look at his comrades, who walked with eyes downcast.

Soon, they were in the ancient burial room of deceased popes. All men stood, with hoods well over their bowed heads. All were silent. They stood like statues in a circle. Their lanterns' flickering lights cast ghostly shadows in the eerie, dark tomb.

The secret initiation took place, and they repeated the Jesuit oath. "I will go to any part of the world, whatsoever, without murmuring and will be submissive in all things whatsoever communicated to me. I do further promise and declare that I will, when opportunity presents, make and wage restless war, through legal legislation and social-media secretly or openly against all heretics, terrorists, Jews, and other dissenters as I am directed to do. I will extirpate through state and church and exterminate them from the face of the earth, as I am directed by any agent of the pope or superior of the brotherhood of the holy faith of the Society of Jesus."

After the initiation, all twenty were individually blessed by the leader of the Society of Jesus as designated by St Ignatius Loyola in the sixteenth century. This was the renewal of the ancient order and their modern secret mission.

## Chapter 1

# Sydney, Australia

Julie stared in excitement at the tall, stately stone building, with its arched pillars and wide verandas. She was attending a weekend workshop for her new chaplains' course. Her husband, a pleasant-looking young man with dark hair and eyes, drove the family's red Pajero through the gates, then up a long driveway that followed a roundabout with a central statue of Mary. They had arrived at their destination, St Mary's Convent, located in Springwood, a town nestled in Sydney's Blue Mountains.

Julie kissed her two children, ten-year-old Beth and six-year-old John, who were in school uniform. With bag in hand, she leaned into the driver's side and kissed her husband, Robert.

"Bye. Take care. Children, please do as Daddy says. I'll only be away for the weekend. Robert, please don't forget to pick me up on Sunday at 4:00 p.m." Then she turned to the children. "Kids, don't let Daddy forget—4:00 p.m., okay?" she reminded them.

"Mum, can we have tea at McDonald's?" asked Beth.

"If Daddy says you can," answered Julie.

She took a deep breath, turned, and entered the foyer. She could hardly contain her excitement, which was tinged with apprehension. Quickly, she swung around to see the family car disappear through the gates. Her multi-coloured peasant skirt flapped in the breeze and clung to her tall, thin frame, and her long, blond hair shone in the afternoon sun.

***She took a deep breath, turned, and entered the foyer. She could hardly contain her excitement, which was tinged with apprehension.***

Father Frank stood in the back corner of the foyer, hidden by the shadows of a wide-arched veranda. He was a tall, thin, dour man who rarely smiled. He was quiet as he watched the new participants meet and chatter excitedly.

A small, thin, elderly woman, smartly dressed, with dyed brown hair and impeccable nails, wrung her hands and sighed nervously as she stepped out of the stairway shadows.

Julie sighted her as she entered the foyer. "Oh, there you are, Janet!" she called. "It's good to see you. I didn't know if I was the first to arrive."

Janet grabbed Julie's arm. "We're sharing a room. It's on the second floor, and it looks over the central courtyard."

"This is an interesting building," Julie responded as they climbed the stairs. She felt excited and thought, *I wonder how the young novice nuns felt, who lived and trained here?*

Janet leaned forward and whispered, "Have you been in a building like this before?"

"No, I haven't."

"I think it's a bit spooky," Janet responded in a shaky whisper.

Julie laughed. "It reminds me of my mother's nursing days. It would have been fun."

They walked together up the wide staircase to a foyer about the size of a large room in a family home. In the right-hand corner was a larger-than-life statue of Mary holding Baby Jesus. The walls were lined with armchairs of different sizes and shapes; they all looked very comfortable. Past this room were two wide corridors: one to the left of the foyer and one straight ahead.

Janet spoke softly. "The nuns' meals were taken in the main dining hall downstairs, but they could take snacks and small personal meals up here. Our dinner will soon be ready."

"I believe it will be quite a feast," Julie replied.

Janet nodded. "Yes, they say so. Our room is straight ahead, halfway down this hall. It's number thirty-five," she added as they walked down the corridor. "The men are up on the third floor."

The room was typical of these institutions. It was large and stark, with two single beds. The walls and the bedspreads were white. The single light shade hanging from the ceiling had once been white but now was yellow with age. The furniture was old and dark. Three tall, narrow windows sat in the stark outer wall. The windows became pictures of colour and beauty as if they were paintings because they framed the flowered courtyard below.

Soon the dinner gong was heard, just as a group of mature-aged students came down the hallway and stopped to introduce themselves.

The next morning, happy chatter over breakfast filled the room. All participants spoke of their anticipated study program with great excitement.

During their first midday break, the students sat at a long table in the central courtyard and chatted under tall, shady trees. Behind was a wall with a gate that led to the nuns' chapel. The wall was covered with sprawling vines and small wisteria flowers. The building's arched verandas faced into this courtyard, giving it a feeling of stability. To one side of the courtyard, a statue of Mary stood in a small man-made cave. In front of it was a garden of impatiens flowers. Amongst the flowers stood a small bench, where attending nuns once sat and prayed.

Pat, a mature, solidly-built, no-nonsense woman with glasses, cleared her voice and spoke to a nun sitting with her. "I've heard nuns came to this statue to pray, and there were many Mary apparitions."

"Yes, that's right," Sister Maria answered. She was a small, elderly person, with dark eyes and typical Italian features, now well-lined with the passage of time. "When I was a novice, I spent my early years in this convent, and Mary told us that in the near future there would be terrible times, and blood would be shed if nations and churches didn't come together in peace." She spoke in a quiet, demure manner with her hands crossed in her lap. All at the table listened. Pat wanted to ask more questions about the apparitions but thought better of it.

In the afternoon class, the students were divided into groups of five. These groups would work for the next year in different hospitals.

Father Frank Finke sat silently in a small lounge room in the convent. The students entered, holding questionnaire sheets and graphs. This was their first training session.

Father Frank spoke as he lounged in a comfortable corner chair. "You have all had time to answer the questions and complete the graph. You will take turns introducing yourselves. Then I want you to explain your graph and how it showed personal issues and insights. What you have discovered will help you understand others in a crisis. Janet, could you introduce yourself and then explain the highs and lows on your graph," Father Frank snapped.

"My name is Janet Smith, and my husband, Albert, is a retired police officer. We have two children. We have an adult son Brad and a teenage daughter Anita. Well, my graph showed that my life was trouble-free until my mother's sudden death. This happened when I was a teenager."

"Could you tell us how this affected you?" Father Frank prompted.

She didn't respond.

"Tell us about it," he gruffly urged.

"Well," she stammered, "it was terrible. I needed my mother." Now tearful, she continued. "I suppose it still upsets me when I stop and think about it," she sobbed into her handkerchief and refused to go on.

Father Frank continued talking to the class. "You can see why we need to face our grief; it's so we can understand others when they're grieving," he explained in a monotone. "Julie, you're next!"

Blond, curly-haired Julie, with her sparkling blue eyes and a deep-dimpled sunny smile, spoke. "My graph showed I had a happy childhood." Her charismatic personality and beliefs seemed to aggravate him. He just moved onto the next person in the circle without listening to any more of her story.

"Pat Bailey," he said and curled his lip in a sneer. "Your graph—what does it tell you?"

"Well, my graph started out rocky when I was a baby because I spent most of my first year in a hospital. While there, if people touched me, it was to give me painful penicillin injections, and when I was brought home, Mum found it hard to bond with me in that first year. When I went to school, I learned about Jesus, and things became much better for me from then on."

"Your mother never loved you," Father Frank snapped.

Pat sat there, shocked. It was like someone had slapped her face. "That's not true," she replied, upset.

"Yes, it is, and you know it," he said in a watchful manner. "You have felt all your life you were not loved."

Pat wiped her eyes with her sleeve and stared at him, shocked. He watched her closely and continued with the next person. "Len, tell us about your graph."

"Well, my graph looked fine until I came to Australia from England. I felt so lost that I ended up studying and becoming a Buddhist."

"And did it help?" Father Frank asked.

"Yes," said Len, and dropped his head and said no more.

"We have one more to go; it's our nun, Sister Maria Regazzi, who works at the Inner-City Mission. Sister Maria, tell us about your graph," he asked.

"Well, my graph did a big dive when I left home to become a nun."

"You thought nobody liked you," he snapped.

"No, that's not so. I missed my large Italian family."

"You thought nobody liked you," he bullied.

"No! That's not so, Frank."

Frank looked around and noticed the furious looks from the others in the class. He stood, walked to the door, and silently opened it, and walked away. The participants rose, and without speaking, left the room.

Sister Maria stood and quietly looked out the window. She thought about Frank and how he conducted his class. She had realised something was amiss when she saw knowing looks pass between him and Len. She was certain they shared a secret, but what was it?

She thought of her Italian family. She remembered living in a large old crumbling farmhouse near Goulburn, south of the Blue Mountains. It was after the Second World War, and Italian immigrants travelled to Australia by the shipload back then.

With several other immigrant families, her parents rented an old farmhouse. Each family had one room, and they shared the large old kitchen, bathroom, and laundry. The women worked in the vegetable gardens and shared everything with each other. It was communal living at its best; all were brought together through poverty and a strange new culture.

They were happy, carefree days. The kids would swim in the river that passed through their back yard. She could still see the boys swinging from a rope. "Don't push," she would squeal when it was her turn, but they would, and the boys would laugh heartily when she swung across the river. She then had to jump and swim back to the bank. The laughter and fun came back vividly to her.

She remembered the loaves of bread and home-made spaghetti her mother cooked in huge pots to feed everyone. She could still, after all these years, remember the wonderful pungent odour of fresh herbs and garlic filling the kitchen and all of the house. Yes, she still missed her childhood extended family. She now realised why in her later years, the City Mission had become her family. It was home for her.

On her way home, Sister Maria stepped from the city train and passed streetwalkers in high boots, with short skirts, and heavy makeup. They leaned against shop walls, chewing gum. With sad, hardened faces, they watched passing cars and people with caution. It was the middle of the day, and they were at work. Nobody cared or sent them on their way.

Sister Maria passed a video shop where mothers with their small children were choosing movies about the spirit world, the occult, or outer space—all happy with what they were doing. Farther on, she passed an Internet games shop with posters on its windows, showing action-packed games with characters that looked like demons. Children and youth crowded these shops, spending their money on demonic concepts and war games with music that beat into their brains through earphones that seemed glued to their heads.

As Sister Maria entered the city mission, she felt very depressed. *What has this world come to?* She wondered. She sighed and sat down, closing her eyes.

# Chapter 2

# Club of Rome

The phone rang in the office of St Mary's Convent in Springwood. "Hello, this is Father Frank Finke. Yes. Yes. Okay, mm-hmm. One hour at 10:00 a.m. Yes, that would be fine. Yes, that's okay. Goodbye."

Father Frank stared through the window, across the convent's grounds of uncleared bushland. Tall gums, with lantana, and tufts of dry grass under trees covered the unkempt areas, and many small dirt paths meandered through the bush toward the creek. He didn't notice his surroundings that morning as he stood thinking about recent developments between the governments of the world and his pope.

As he mused, a large black Mercedes drove through the convent gates and stopped at the front entrance at exactly the time stated. Two men stepped out, and the driver drove to the specified car park and waited.

"Hello, Frank," the elderly priest said, as Father Frank walked toward them. "I wish to introduce you to Cardinal Calvin." They all shook hands. "Do you think you could escort us around the convent's grounds?" the priest requested.

The two men accompanied Father Frank Finke around the ten hectares of bushland that surrounded the gardens and chapel. They looked at Magdala Creek on the eastern boundary of the property. "It's certainly a large, fast-flowing creek," the cardinal remarked. "It will supply us with plenty of water."

"I'll take you to the other side of the property, and you can examine the convent's machinery," Father Frank suggested.

When they came to the other side, they were pleased to see a large vegetable garden, fruit trees, and a substantial amount of machinery in the sheds.

Father Frank escorted the two men to his ground-floor office, where a pot of tea with biscuits awaited them.

Relaxed with his cup of tea, Father Jones, an elderly priest with grey hair and beard, spoke. "How many people can the convent hold?"

"There are fifty twin rooms on both floors, so that would be two hundred people," Father Frank reasoned.

"Yes, I think this property will do," Father Jones said, and he nodded to the others and continued. "A high fence would be easy enough to erect, and there's fresh water and a good cellar, which will be useful. The Australian Government wants to use these old buildings for future detention centres." He placed his cup down and wiped his mouth.

The second person, Cardinal Calvin, who worked with the politicians of the state, spoke with authority. "The world has been divided into ten territories or regions. The world powers within these regions have been asked to come together under the banner of the United Nations Peacekeepers, and all must obey United Nations' decisions."

"Have they passed the new terrorist laws?" Father Frank asked.

"Yes, they have," answered Cardinal Calvin.

Father Frank turned to the elderly priest. "Is this why they want our buildings?"

"Yes, that's correct." The priest nodded and sipped his tea.

Cardinal Calvin continued. "We need all the churches to work together under one banner for the health of the community, and those that cause trouble will be placed in these detention centres."

Father Frank addressed the cardinal with a sly smile. "I believe that the United Nations refers to the cardinals as the 'Club of Rome.'"

The high-ranking priest looked up, shocked. His face hardened for a moment as he stared at Father Frank in disbelief and thought, *Typical tactless Frank; he has no idea of protocol or manners. I've been told he's very callous and has no people skills, but he knows how to get the job done, and we need people like him in administration in these centres.*

"Yes," he answered, "that's what they call us, but they wouldn't say it to our faces." He smirked, nodding to the priest. Both realised Frank missed the prod.

A knock was heard, and a young man entered. Father Frank introduced him. "This is Len. He's been undercover as a Buddhist in our chaplain classes." The men nodded and shook hands.

"Well, I think it would be best if we conducted the ceremony in the church, don't you, Frank?" Father Jones asked.

"Yes, I've unlocked the church," responded Father Frank; then he stood and led the way.

Passing through the neat courtyard with its flowering vines and statue of Mary, they passed out of the gate and along a well-worn path meandering through tall gums to the front entrance of the tiny stone chapel.

The chapel windows, six on each side, had coloured leadlight glass depicting scenes of Calvary. The morning sun shone through these windows, giving the neighbouring pews a soft light and making the window depictions, with their bright colours and clever artwork, consume all other light in the room. At the front was a lifelike stone image of Jesus hanging on a cross, and light passing through the windows danced colour across the stone form.

They walked to the front altar. Cardinal Calvin stood while the young man knelt in front of him, and the others knelt in the front pew. He then anointed and blessed the young man.

After prayers, the young man stood. Cardinal Calvin addressed him. "You are now our undercover Jesuit priest, and you will work at the assigned hospitals. Your work is very important for world peace and its One World Church. You will report to Father Frank at all times. You will obey only his orders, and you will be silent and not share information on your duties with anyone. Have your duties been explained to you?"

***"You are now our undercover Jesuit priest, and you will work at the assigned hospitals. Your work is very important for world peace and its One World Church."***

"Yes, sir," Len answered.

The young man then read out loud the Jesuit oath written on paper.

When the officials left, Father Frank went back into the church and conducted the old, more sinister induction into the secret order as designated by Ignatius Loyola back in the sixteenth century.

In the shadow of the back pew, unknown to those who participated in the initiation, a nun knelt and prayed. She witnessed all that was said and heard the extreme oath of induction into the secret Jesuit order.

## Chapter 3

# Grand Master

Father Frank Finke and the Springwood convent's staff had been busy all afternoon. The grounds were tidied and prepared for the midyear formal event. In the middle of the courtyard was a neat pile of wood with a large wooden cross in its centre. Banners with a half-moon and the sun within hung from the veranda balconies.

At midnight, guests arrived in chauffeur-driven black Mercedes, hired for the evening. All forty men wore white Ku Klux Klan robes and head-gear that covered their faces, with only a gap for their eyes and mouths. They were government officials and public servants from all over Australia. These high-ranking men had been initiated into the Jesuit order, and their identity was an important secret. They were under orders from Rome and would be responsible for future world events that will overthrow the order of things now in place.

Slowly, silently, one by one, they entered the foyer and were given a gold candle holder with six purple, lit candles. Filing into the courtyard, they placed their candle holder and glowing candles on high-stands flanking the courtyard, then stood silently until all forty did the same.

When all were present, the Grand Master watching from the balcony above, held his hand high, giving the Jesuit salute. They followed with the salute and repeated after him the secret Jesuit creed.

The Grand Master lifted his hand, telling them to sit. He sat on his purple throne chair and proceeded with his speech. "One of our symbols, the sun inside the moon, can be seen displayed throughout nations of the world."

He continued. "There is a handful of people who control and own the world. They are financiers, princes, and prime ministers, presidents, and important world leaders, and all are thirty-three-degree Freemasons. They are affiliated with us. These men are very rich and own the banks, industries, and nations. We are working together for the future One World Government."

Resting back in his comfortable throne chair, he continued. "Before the Second World War, the Jews were leaders in world banking, industry, and also culture. As in the past, they kept their wealth amongst their own. We had to do something about it before they completely destroyed our agenda; so, we staged the war, and then the Jewish camps to rid ourselves of the vermin."

All the while, tall, slender, scantily-dressed girls with high-heeled shoes and party masks served the men alcoholic beverages. One stood with tray in hand, serving the Grand Master. He continued. "We are responsible for sinking the Titanic. Some of the richest families were on board, and once again, we had to take care of the economy, making sure it was as we planned. We were behind John Kennedy's death because he refused to obey us, and we programmed the attack on the World Trade Centre in New York. We blamed Islamic people and said it was a terrorist attack. This allowed us to establish new terrorist laws, which, in turn, have changed America's constitution for religious freedom. These new laws will allow us to arrest and imprison people before they are proven guilty."

The men below listened intently. The Grand Master continued. "We have overthrown the Protestant world with the ecumenical movement. It took many centuries to infiltrate into the first Christian church, but the movements have been much more rapid this time and have only taken about half a century to mingle the Eastern philosophies and the occult with Christianity. Everything is now in place to take over the world."

He stood and leaned over the balcony, making sure his words were heard. "We have developed a virus to take over the world in plague proportions. It is in progress now. The people of the world are being tested, groomed, so to speak, and martial law will be a normal event for them. There will be isolation and bondage because of the virus and new government laws. This is now taking place, and the take-over of the world is nearly completed."

A roar went up from the drunken Jesuits below. The bonfire was lit, and bottles were thrown at the cross with many satanic curses. Satan gloated as his plan to take over the world was soon to take place.

## Chapter 4

# Chatsworth–Midnight

Anita, Janet and Albert's daughter, was staying at Aunt Linda's home with her cousin Jenny. The girls had sneaked out and were roaming the streets and—*well*—

"Anita, walk a little faster, or we'll miss our bus," Jen called.

Anita ran towards her cousin, laughing. "Hey! Jenny," she whispered. "The graveyard back there." She leaned over to check her watch in the street light and continued. "Well, there's something going on in there. I saw dark shadows and heard people talking."

"Let's go back," Jenny giggled. "It may be Jazz and Fran. They said something about visiting a graveyard at midnight with their teacher, Miss Lenard. Maybe it was this graveyard. Let's sneak back and see what's going on."

"Yeah, but it's past midnight. Shoot, there goes our bus! Now we've got to walk home!" Anita exclaimed, not impressed. She felt scared in Chatsworth's suburb, especially when alone with Jenny at this late hour. She stamped her feet and jumped around in circles. "Shoot, shoot, shoot," she shouted in mock rage.

"Stupid," giggled Jenny tugging on Anita's arm. "Come on, let's go, but stop calling out, or they'll hear us."

The two ran back giggling and half-crouching as they approached the old Chatsworth Cemetery gates. In the moonlight they could clearly see large, old gravestones standing tall, like ghostly statues. Then they spotted movement. Dark shadows seemed to move on the other side of the cemetery. They could hear voices, and then there was a light. The shadows now became people who slid into a car. The car's lights suddenly beamed into trees and lit up the road as the engine purred and the car moved forward along the sleepy street.

"Blow, we'll never know who it was," Anita yelled.

"Be quiet, Anita. You're going to wake people and get the cops called again. Mum said she'll tell your dad next time it happens."

"I can't help it," Anita said, still giggling. "It's all the Ecstasy we popped at the rave party—but I want to know who was in the graveyard," she squealed, more quietly now, and jumped up and down. "Now, we'll never know."

"Yes, we will. Jazz and Fran are good mates of mine. They'll tell us. Just don't worry about a thing," Jenny laughed. She ran along, scraping a large stick against the fences. The din woke dogs, which barked furiously, and the owners yelled at them from their bedrooms. Lights went on and off intermittently. Some houses had sensor lights that now bathed the front yards.

"Now who's noisy?" Anita called as they ducked down a dim side street, now walking quietly. She was scared, as the street had few lights and was mostly dark. Both knew this was a dangerous district, and this street was especially so at such a late hour. As they watched, dark shadows moved around the house yards. They hid themselves next to trees until the shadows had moved down the street. These night people were a well-known gang that raided homes in this district.

Soon Anita and Jenny were back on the main highway. They walked past the bus stop, as there wasn't another bus for hours. Coming to a car partly parked on the footpath, the girls looked around. "Here it comes," Jenny yelled. A rock crashed through the side window.

"Oh, no, Jenny! You naughty girl!" Anita laughed.

Both girls scrambled into the car and looked for money. They found about ten dollars in the ashtray, and then suddenly, a taxi came from nowhere. He pulled up just in front of the car the girls were raiding. Slipping out of the passenger-side door, they hoped the cabby didn't notice they had been in the car.

His side window opened, and he called, "Anita, Jenny, hop in; I'll give you a ride home."

"It's Mr. Wilkinson," Jenny whispered. "We're in for a lecture."

"I hope he doesn't talk to our folks," Anita whispered back.

"Girls, have a good look at the car behind us," Mr. Wilkinson said as they slid across the back seat. Anita and Jenny turned, and in the street light, they could see the broken window. "Did you see who did that?"

"No," they both answered.

"You're very lucky I happened along. There's a gang breaking into homes and cars in this area. I must ring the police and alert them of their whereabouts." Mr. Wilkinson proceeded to hit his mobile keypad. "Yes, it's them alright," he said to the questioning cops.

"Sure, sure," whispered Jenny, in the back seat. "It's all put on to scare us," she said to an already sleeping Anita.

* * *

The next morning, standing in the front yard of the local Chatsworth State High School were four young girls dressed in black clothes, with heavy black eyeliner, black nails, and black hair that hung down over one eye—though one girl wore a bright pink stripe of colour through her dyed hair. They all wore many metal rings in their faces.

Parents passed and muttered to each other. One lady spoke loudly to her friend. "I think it's disgraceful that the school doesn't enforce the dress code; after all, there is a uniform they're supposed to wear."

Jenny, who wore the heaviest makeup in her Goth group and sported the bold pink stripe in her hair, laughed loudly at the story Fran and Jazz were telling her. "So, it was you two at the graveyard? You must tell us about it."

Anita tugged at Jenny's arm as a police car slowly drove into the school's front car park. "Let's go to class," she whispered.

They had started math when a police officer and the headmaster entered the classroom. The headmaster spoke quietly to the teacher.

"Could Jenny Green and Anita Smith please step out of the room?" The teacher called.

They were taken to the headmaster's office. *We're in for it now,* Jenny thought.

"I believe you were being followed last night," the police officer said. "Could you please tell me what you noticed about the car and the occupants?"

Jenny breathed a sigh of relief. Mr. Wilkinson had swallowed her story. She happily answered the police officer's questions. Anita sat quietly, not game enough to enter the conversation. It might be recorded, and she didn't want her father to find out.

## Chapter 5

# Linda's Home

Janet had received a phone call early that morning from Linda. Janet was to let herself into Linda's home. The key was under the potted plant at the front door. Her sister explained that she would be home sometime later as she had to work an emergency shift at the Sydney Hospital, but the girls should be there after school.

Janet arrived at her sister's First World War bungalow early that afternoon. It was on a street at Chatsworth with other such homes that were old and scruffy. It had paint peeling off the veranda posts and half concrete walls. Linda had placed brightly-flowering potted plants along the veranda walls, trying to cheer up the drab exterior. The yard was as drab. The garden had a few weedy patches of flowers, and where one would have lawn, the yard was paved. Actually, most of the yard had pavers. Janet looked around and thought, *Well, I suppose it would be scruffy. Linda works and doesn't have a husband to help keep the yard clean.*

She let herself in and was surprised how homely and neat Linda kept the inside. The walls were painted a soft lemon colour, and the old timber floors were polished. Her sister had stitched beautiful tapestries that hung on the walls throughout the house. *Linda has always been the clever one with her hands. She's just like Mum when she was alive,* she thought.

In the kitchen was a large fish tank with rocks and reeds and bright, colourful tropical fish. Across from this was the computer. *I dare say this is where the girls do their homework,* she thought as she passed through the kitchen's back door into the enclosed porch-cum-laundry.

The girls' large back bedroom came off this porch. She was told the girls would have it locked, but she was curious and tried the handle, and the door opened.

What a shock! Clothes lay on the carpet where they had been dropped. Clothes lay on top of cupboards, draped off chairs, and were flung over bed rails. The black-painted walls were covered with posters of Goth idols. A quilt in its bright red satin cover was flung in a corner, and the bed unmade. The second bed was the same. Anita's violin case was empty.

CDs with no cases, CD cases with no CDs were flung about the room. Teen magazines lay amongst makeup and hairbrushes. Dirty bath towels that would have been wet when flung there lay amongst dry clothes. On closer inspection neat piles of clean clothes were left on the floor with dirty. *Surely Anita wouldn't live like this. She was always so particular when home!* But it was Anita's mess, as well as her cousin's.

Janet stood there shocked. *I am so glad Albert doesn't know about my visit. He would be furious if he knew what was going on, and he wouldn't let Anita forget this mess*.

Janet sat quietly in the lounge room, waiting for the girls to come home from school. She didn't know what she was going to say or do and felt quite ill with the worry of it all. Usually, Albert took care of the children's behaviour problems, but she had promised her sister not to tell.

Now plucking at her cardigan nervously, she thought. *How could Anita let her down like this? Anita had been sheltered, but she was such a good girl when they all lived at Chatsworth. She only mixed with studious kids back then. Anita had asked her to get permission from Albert to live with Aunty Linda so she could be with her friends at her old school. She said it would be too hard to start a new school in her final year. She was now only halfway through the first term of school, so what had happened to her old friends? I wish we hadn't left the area until Anita's education was finished, and why did I leave Anita with my sister Linda.*

As she sat and thought about these things, she looked around at the tapestries, and memories of her mother came back sharply. She really missed her mother, and sadness flooded over her. Tears fell, and she dabbed at her eyes. Eventually, the stress made her weary, and she dropped off to sleep.

Voices at the door woke her. Linda and the girls walked past the lounge room into the kitchen. Jenny was yelling at her mother. "Yeah, sure thing, Mum, whatever you say."

"Jenny, I know I'm not always home, but you've been told about roaming the streets. It's so dangerous! Look what happened to you last night."

"Yeah, yeah, anything you like, Mum. Come on, Anita, we don't have to listen to this. Let's go over to Jazz's place. Her mum is stoned most of the time, so she doesn't have to put up with this garbage." She turned to her mother. "If you like, we'll go to Melbourne with Jazz. She said she's going to her dad's, as she hates her mother." She looked over at Anita, who stared back in shock. Jenny screamed at the top of her voice, "I hate you, Mum."

Linda screamed back. "Don't be stupid, Jenny. I let you do whatever you want. Why would you want to leave? You have it really good here. How would you survive without money?"

Janet opened her mouth to reply when another voice spoke. It was a familiar male voice, and it sounded very angry.

"That's the problem, Linda; you never had boundaries. You should've had rules a long time ago."

It was Albert; he had been listening at the open front door, and he didn't look impressed. He walked into the kitchen, looking like he had just entered a drug raid. Even though Anita could see her father was furious, she walked over to him; he placed his arm around her shoulders. She stood with her arms around his large, wide waist, looking up at him, with tears rolling unchecked down her face, leaving smudgy black makeup on her cheeks.

"I have it on good authority the girls are dabbling in drugs. Last night they went to a rave party and took a cocktail of drugs." Looking down at Anita. "You'll be coming home with us."

Walking out to the girls' room, Albert stood there silent for a moment and then started yelling. "Get in here this minute, Anita." He looked at the dishevelled bedroom—a reflection of the girls' state of mind as far as he was concerned.

"Linda, get me the clippers! I know you have them in your bathroom—and you, young lady," he said to his daughter. "Come with me."

He made Anita scrub her face. Her face became grey as black makeup mixed with soap. She rinsed her face, not game to argue. Never before had she seen her father this angry.

Pushing her down on a chair, he shaved off her hair. All the women in the house were crying, but none moved or interfered with what was happening.

When finished, he spoke to his daughter. "Next week, young lady, you will be going to a drug rehab centre for three weeks, and then you will complete your final year of school at Springwood High."

## Chapter 6

# New Hope Retreat

Mist-covered mountains surrounded the valley in the Blue Mountains of Sydney. Here the New Hope Retreat sat, with its dormitories nestled on wide green lawns among tall gum trees.

Anita had completed her early morning yoga class, and now with twenty other guests, sat quietly on her meditation mat. The air was fresh, and the early morning breeze was invigorating. The only sound was the high-pitched tinkling, like a thousand small bells, from bellbirds that surrounded the retreat.

In this session Anita was told to clear her mind of all things; to just sit, breathe deeply, and feel and absorb her surroundings. She did this, and as she relaxed, God's great love flooded her mind. How could she sit there, in the midst of nature, among such tranquillity and breathtaking beauty, and not think of the world's Creator? Her mother had taken her regularly to church, and she was grateful for a second chance. Soon, the breakfast bell broke the silence, and people stood, stretched, smiled, and quietly gathered their things.

The breakfast room was warm and filled with wonderful aromas. Everyone was starving. They had just come off a ten-day fast. First, they had juices for five days, and then raw foods for another five; now, they were about to eat their first cooked, hot meal, and it smelled fantastic.

Soon, Anita's stay would be over, and she felt reluctant to leave. She felt she couldn't face the world out there. She had kept to herself but was impressed with a young male counsellor. He had a kind word for everyone and was thoughtful and always ready to help. Anita saw him in many different places, praying with people. It was an Ashram retreat, yet he prayed without interference. He wasn't ashamed or embarrassed about his faith.

Tommy really impressed her. Perhaps it was his quiet strength that turned her eye—something that at the moment, she was positive she lacked. She was cross with herself and her weak character. *I'm a crowd follower,* she thought.

After the meal, she was to attend Tommy's lecture, and today it was her turn to talk about her problems. She had kept putting it off, but today was the day, and she had to face it.

Anita lay on her bed; she wasn't going to class. No way was she going to talk about the reason she was at the retreatnot to anybody, but especially not to Tommy. What would he think of her? No, she wouldn't tell anybody. She was determined about it, and in frustration, flung her scarf across the bed. The silly thing was making her head itch, but she wasn't letting anyone see her shaved head, that was now growing into blond prickles. Ashamed, she didn't want to explain the reason for her latest hairstyle. Anita realised some people at the centre thought she had cancer, as many who were afflicted with life-threatening diseases and health problems came to the cleansing programs. Now, feeling cross and defiant, Anita lay with her eyes shut.

Lila, the centre's domestic help, entered Anita's room. She had thought all the guests were at the lecture. She stood, quietly watching the girl. Was she ill? Did she need help?

She spoke in a concerned manner. "Can I get somebody to help you, dear?"

Anita hadn't heard the domestic enter her room and jumped up quickly, grabbing her scarf and swiftly wrapping it turban-style around her head, but it was too late.

The old lady had seen her shaved head but pretended she hadn't. "Can I get you help, dear?" she asked once again.

"No," Anita replied stubbornly.

The woman hesitated for a moment or two. "If you're not ill, you must attend class, lass. I will need to report you if you don't go," she explained.

Anita swung her legs over the bed and thumped her feet down on the floor. She clutched at her turban, tugging it tightly on her head, then stood and marched out of the room.

As she walked down the passage, she could hear a male voice conducting class. Standing in front of the open door, she could see the lecturer had a bald head with grey tufts of hair around the edges. He was very large framed. *It's Dr. Jones,* thought Anita. *Where is Tommy?*

She looked at the others, who were concentrating on a girl, who was crying and talking, and there he was. Tommy had positioned himself opposite the door. When he saw her, his eyebrows went up, and a relieved smile crossed his face. He was concerned and had been waiting for her.

Anita's heart jumped. She felt embarrassed and unsure. She spun on her heels and went through the double door opposite the lecture room into the meditation room. Flopping on a seat, she felt hot and snatched off her turban. She rubbed her now sweaty fingers hard into her scalp. "How embarrassing," she whispered out loud to herself.

She leaned forward, saw a pair of feet, and looked up to see Tommy standing there. He gently pushed past her knees and sat next to her.

Tommy noticed how her short, fair, prickled hair accentuated her delicate features and large blue eyes. *She's so beautiful,* he thought.

Tears welled and flowed down Anita's cheeks. Tommy wriggled about, trying to retrieve something from his pocket, and handed her his handkerchief. He was tempted to wipe her tears himself but thought better of it. It was at this moment Anita realised she was homesick, and she wished her dad was there as she could do with a big hug.

Tommy leaned forward and picked up her hand, and patted it gently. "It always helps if you share your problems," he said very gently.

She sobbed out loud. His kind, caring voice brought all the pain of the last few months to the surface.

Tommy continued. "You can tell me. I hear all sorts of things in here. Once it's off your chest, you'll feel better, and then the healing process will start."

Anita told him about her drug ordeal and her misbehaviour while at her Auntie Linda's home. "I'm so ashamed of the things I did."

"What happened to your friends?"

"Jill and Anne were twin sisters. They were killed in a car accident over the school holidays. I only found out when I went back to school, and I miss them terribly," she wept.

***Daniel and the others in the Bible stood true only by standing with their God. It's only possible to be strong through prayer and walking daily with your Lord.***

"When you're lonely and sad, do you make it a habit to do drugs?"

"Of course not!" Anita replied indignantly.

"When you were with Jill and Anne, did they make all the decisions, and you just followed?"

Anita pondered for a moment. "No, I think it was equal. Yes, I know where you're going with this. Why did I let my cousin lead me astray? Well, thinking about it, I think I did it for peace. There wasn't anything but fights over there. Jenny was such a hostile person. She really scared me." She started to cry again. "I'm so ashamed; I thought I was stronger than that. You know, a Daniel standing ever so true and all of that stuff."

"Well, Daniel and the others in the Bible stood true only by standing with their God. It's only possible to be strong through prayer and walking daily with your Lord. This is how, and only how, we can stay strong, Anita. We're asked to repent, which you have done, and now you must accept Jesus' forgiveness. Cheer up—treat it as a learning curve. Not a good one, but I'm sure it's one you won't repeat. Would you like me to pray with you?" he asked kindly.

"Yes, please," replied Anita timidly.

* * *

While lining up at the food counter, Tommy whispered as he bumped against Anita's arm, "Hello! We meet again."

She giggled. "Tommy, you must spend more time with the other guests. I'm sure they need you as well."

He grinned. "I'll make a bargain with you. You can get me whatever you're eating, and I'll meet you back at the table. I have some people I have to see."

Anita piled her plate with many different types of salads, placing it on a table near the counter, and then proceeded to do the same for Tommy. When she had completed her task, she looked up to see where he had gone. She caught his eye, and he gave her a big wink. The people he was talking with turned around to see who he was winking at. Anita dropped her head in embarrassment and pretended to arrange the cutlery on the table.

* * *

The three weeks passed, and it was time to go home. Anita and Tommy stood together outside her dormitory, waiting for Anita's parents. When they arrived, Anita rushed to their car.

"Boy! I missed you both," she said as she hugged them. She turned to Tommy. "Dad and Mum, I would like you to meet my friend, Tommy."

Albert's thick eyebrows puckered together, a habit he had when he wasn't pleased. "Well, I suppose you're still at high school?" he asked Tommy.

"No, Mr. Smith, I go to Sydney University, and I have just completed my practicum here at the retreat for my sociology degree."

"Well! I'm glad to hear that." Albert smiled, offering his hand to Tommy. Tommy understood Albert's concern for his daughter and shook his hand.

## Chapter 7

# Kundalini

Janet and Albert Smith lived on five hectares at Springwood in the Blue Mountains, in a modern timbered Australian homestead, with a brick chimney and large verandas that commanded breathtaking views down a steep valley. Behind the property was a tall, majestic mountain, with early-morning mist covering its rugged terrain.

Janet sat on the veranda dressed warmly in a thick tracksuit. She wrapped her hands around a warm cup of tea and blew steam from her breath into the cold air. She watched her husband, a tall, solid, middle-aged man with dark, balding hair and thick brows that knitted together when he frowned, as he often did these days, silently feeding local kookaburra that had flown in from the bush.

Janet thought of her classes and the horrible Father Frank. She thought of her mother, and she thought of her daughter Anita and hoped she had learned her lesson. Anita's friend Tommy from the "New Hope Retreat" seemed a nice person, with a strong personality. Perhaps she saw something in him that reminded her of her father. She had always adored her father.

Janet watched the early morning news in the kitchen. The news displayed the scenes on the TV. The reporter read. "Family breakdown and community lawlessness are at epidemic proportions. Young teenagers in Sydney and other parts of Australia are out of control. We are seeing more and more violent home invasions, car hi-jacking, and drug deaths at festivals committed by these young teenagers.'

Max Hiller returned to the screen. "The pope is visiting countries of the world to introduce a new green deal with a family rest day as part of the program. He has made arrangements for 100 countries to visit the Vatican to sign a global pact that will bring in educational reform for the youth of the world."

The door chimes rang and voices in the hall could be heard. It was Brad talking to their visitor. He was home from his Terrorist Peace Corps duties. "You're on time, mate, but I don't know if my sleepy sister is up yet," he said as he stepped aside to let Tommy in.

"Hello, Tommy," said Janet as she met the boys in the kitchen. "Would you like breakfast before you go?"

Albert, who had started his breakfast and had his mouth full, looked up from his morning paper, grunted, and nodded.

"Good morning, Mr. Smith," Tommy responded.

"Sit here, Tommy," said Janet as she placed toast and jam in front of him.

"Thanks," he said as he sat. He was about to speak when Anita bounded into the room and butted in.

"Hi, Tommy," and to the others in the room, "It looks as if we're going to have a nice day." She kissed her father's bald head and continued, "Dad, Brad's going to take us to the gospel hall. All the churches congregate together for worship in this hall."

"One of those churches," Albert grunted, with a shake of his head. "You know I don't approve of all their carrying on, but you go if you want to."

"There, there, dear, it can't be too bad. Billy Jones is preaching, and he's a famous evangelist," Janet said in a small, timid voice while patting her husband's shoulder to pacify him.

"Well, he's as stupid as the rest," he snorted.

"Well, dear, I must admit, I was surprised when Brad told me about it," she agreed.

"Ha!" Albert responded with brows drawn together. "It's a lot of nonsense if you ask me. It's best to keep to the old traditions," he said and went back to his paper.

Anita was scared but excited when they pulled into the car park at the gospel hall. She didn't know what to expect. Tommy went along with it but wasn't happy as it was against the stand he and his family made with their church congregation. They came out of a similar type of worship to keep the truths of the Bible, but he thought Anita needed to see for herself where the churches were heading.

As they walked to the hall, Brad, a stereotypical police officer with short brown hair and muscled body, explained his duties. "I'm on duty as an usher, but I must tell you the real reason they hire us blokes is to act as bouncers. When anybody causes problems, we take care of the matter and escort them to the watch house."

Anita was really scared now, and she whispered to Tommy.

"Don't worry," Tommy whispered back, "Brad is here, and he will take care of us."

They sat near the entrance at the back of the hall where Brad stood. The hall was already crowded, and it was still quite early. People were excited and laughed and chatted amongst themselves. It didn't seem like church but more like a rock concert with young, trendy teenagers sitting as close to the front as they could.

The famous band from America, the Rock Demons, assembled their instruments. They played at a loud pitch, and the congregation swayed, jumped, and sang to the music. Their shouts and screams competed with loud drums. This went on for about thirty minutes.

Then a middle-aged lady came on stage. She wore bright clothes and makeup. When she raised her hands, the band lowered their music to a quiet beat.

"We have come to call Kundalini the serpent. We must call him out. He is coiled in your spine," she screamed. The woman jumped up and down and waved her hands above her head, and the people followed. The drum volume picked up, and soon, the young people began to fall to the ground, writhing and slithering in serpent-like movements. They were unable to stand. They screamed and screamed.

Tommy and Anita, in shock, held hands and closed their eyes in prayer. They realised they shouldn't be there.

When all was completely quiet, the famous preacher, Billy Jones from America, came on stage. He wore a white suit. He raised his hands and formed the goat symbol that represented Satan. He prayed and then began his sermon.

"In this audience, we have all denominations present. They have been encouraged to assemble together. We have come together in love. Love brings unity. You, the audience, are sovereign and your needs are to be recognised, recognised over individual doctrines. We, as a church, need to understand this. The needs of the community must come first; they must be satisfied."

He continued, "We have many doctrines amongst us because we're from many denominations, but love comes first. We must first love ourselves so that we can love others. God is eternal love. We are made in God's image, and if we can love like He does, we will be like God." He waved his hands in the air and walked back and forth on the stage.

"Let's pray," he said. "We pray to You, God our Father, for unity with all churches and the community. Help us to put the community's needs before our own church doctrines. We now ask you, Lord, to bring your people forward in dedication. Amen."

"Come, children! Come up and receive the Holy Spirit!" he called.

Many stepped forward and stood quietly at the front. The band played softly. When all who were coming came, the band stopped. Pastor Billy Jones then placed his hands on the people and one by one, at his command, they fell backward.

"Receive the Holy Spirit!" he yelled as one fell. He continued, "You are slain in the Spirit!" Then he said to the next person, "You are healed by the Holy Ghost!" and he yelled to the next and the next and so on, as they each fell backward in the arms of a church servant. Some fell to the floor.

Large collection buckets were passed back and forth while they sang gospel songs, and most felt compelled to place large donations in these buckets.

# Chapter 8

# People of the Night

That afternoon a group of friends went with Anita and Tommy to the Inner-City Mission's kitchen to help Sister Maria with her evening meal. They wore large aprons that Sister Maria provided and chopped soup vegetables quickly as they discussed the morning service. While they spoke, Pat and Julie entered the room to help with the preparations.

"What's all the excitement?" Julie asked with a broad smile.

"Julie, you know how we talked in the past about spiritualism? Well, we've been told that people are getting real answers from the dead. Some people's dead relatives give messages through spirit mediums about their death or murder. Many times, police find the murderer from these leads. Families who experience this swear it's their family member speaking to them. It seems to give them such relief and even closure."

"Yes, even government officials go to spirit mediums to receive information on how to rule their country," Julie added.

"But why do such a thing?" Anita responded.

"My minister told me about this. It's Satan deluding them," Tommy said. He raised his head and smiled as he looked over at Anita, who stopped chopping vegetables and stood with her knife held in the air, and mouth open. She was obviously in shock.

He continued. "Today, people really believe in these things. Satan knows if he can get them to believe his evil angels are spirits talking to them, he will win, and the people will carry out his grand movements in the end, with spirits manifesting themselves everywhere."

A gangly, blond-headed, Aboriginal street kid about fifteen years old, known as Jacky, entered the kitchen and joined in. "Ah! That's nuthin'. Ya wanna see the night folk call on spirits? Just come with me after tucker. I'll take ya there."

Jacky led Anita and Tommy past the wharves at Sydney Harbour, where the ferries docked and onto the Circular Quay walkway. The Harbour bustled with activity as the busy ferries and hydrofoils returned to the wharves. One kilometre further down, the famous Sydney Harbour Bridge could be seen. Its huge, arched-frame crossed the massive waterway, carrying traffic whose lights glowed in the evening twilight. Ahead was the famous Opera House. Its roof of many peaks represented sails of ships in the harbour. Its beauty startled them. Across from the Opera House was the Royal Botanic Gardens' massive park.

In the park were raggedy, homeless street people of all ages, known as "creatures of the night." They sat cross-legged with hands held high and eyes closed. A hum went up, first low and quiet, then it became louder and louder until all were engulfed in the sound.

"Ommmmmmm … ommmmmm … ommmmm …" Everything else became quiet and still, as the sound surrounded all in the park and those close by.

"Ommmmmm … ommmmm … ommmmmm …"

Suddenly, a strong wind rushed down the wharf, covering an area about ten metres wide, and blew across the heads of those in the park. They tumbled over in its strength and were powerless to rise while it roared and shook over them. The noise was loud and terrible, and within the noise, harsh voices could be heard as spirits yelled and blasphemed terrible things against God. These were the spirits of darkness that controlled these people.

The wind went as quickly as it came, and a short while later, the sound of a chopper in the far distance could be heard. As it approached, it beamed lights down on the stricken street people, as it hovered like a black hawk above its prey.

"Go home now, or action will be taken!" yelled a voice over a loudspeaker. "Go home now! Do you hear? Get yourselves out of here, or action will be taken!"

The street people disappeared into the night as if they had never been there.

Anita and Tommy huddled together in the shadows of the Opera House, frightened beyond belief. When the people and the police in the helicopter disappeared, they came out and moved with Jacky along the wharf toward the highway.

* * *

As they walked in the direction of the highway, they met an old man that was obviously one of them from the park, or was he? He stood on a small box, and with a very strong voice for an old, frail man, he started to preach.

"In heaven, Lucifer was an anointed cherub. He was highly exalted and was greatly loved by the heavenly beings, and his influence over them was strong. When he turned against God, many of the heavenly beings listened to his suggestions and believed his words, and because of this, there was war in heaven. Lucifer's angels fought against God's angels, and they were cast out to earth. Lucifer, known as Satan, set up his kingdom in this world and ever since, has strived to seduce human beings from their allegiance to God. Through Satan's influence, men joined with one another to place their evil influence on others."

He held his arms outstretched and shook his hands in the air. "Satan hates men because Christ died for them, so they can go to heaven. Satan knows he is doomed and will never be accepted back, so he is determined to corrupt and destroy man's chance of being saved!" he called.

Two men walked quickly up to the old man and dragged him to a police car, pushed him in, and drove off.

# Chapter 9

# Terrorist

Albert breathed deeply, savouring the crisp morning air as he looked down the valley below. It was very beautiful with its mist-covered terrain and the mountain behind hidden in fog. The kookaburras visiting the back veranda waited for their morning feed. With his hand, he shielded his eyes from the autumn sun. It was Monday, and he needed to hurry and get ready for work. Albert had come out of retirement for six months to relieve the sergeant at his old police station.

Janet sat in their warm kitchen, watching TV while she ate breakfast. On the early morning news, the commentator announced as footage was shown.

"After a major tip-off, several British terrorists of Middle-Eastern descent have been captured in a siege at London's Central Railway Station. Five men with bags of ammunition were apprehended when they entered the Liverpool morning express. United Nations police stopped another three on escalators trying to escape. It is believed some of the Islamic men managed to get away. It was part of a worldwide operation to cripple railway stations in major cities; never before has such a large-scale terrorist operation been organised. The tip-off enabled the United Nations Terrorist Task Force to be on alert and arrest suspects worldwide. Sydney Central Railway Station is also on high alert this morning." As the commentator read, film clips were shown of the arrests.

"This Max Hiller for Australia Broadcasting Live News."

Sister Maria Regazzi, on the early morning shift at Sydney's Inner-City Mission, rushed through the under-ground tunnel connected to Sydney's Kings Cross Railway Station. In the dim light, she almost tripped on a bundle of rags that smelt of booze.

A head emerged from the rags with groans and curses. "What do ya think ya doin'?" slurred the deep voice of old Walter.

"Sorry, mate. Do you know where the kids are?" She looked at him with sadness. She thought to herself about his situation. *After a party, while quite drunk, he had driven his car into a tree, and all his family were killed. Poor Walter has never forgiven himself. If only he knew Jesus, his pain would be easier to bear.*

"I bet you're hungry," she said in a gentle manner.

He struggled to stand. She helped him.

"Nice hot porridge for you, Walter, at the mission," she smiled.

Walter hobbled in the direction of his regular handout, not seeing the thin, dark shadow that followed Sister Maria. It ducked into side alleys and corners to avoid being sighted.

She continued through the tunnel, up the stairs to the railway station's bright lights with its activity and movement swelling. McDonald's and other shops were preparing breakfast.

She followed a small passage with toilet signage and gave three quick knocks on the door marked "Mothers and Babies." A small, wide-eyed girl of twelve years unlocked the door. She stepped aside, and Maria noticed she had four younger girls with her. They were curled up like little kittens on a large, long, padded seat.

With a soft voice, she spoke to the little girl. "Rosie, your charges seem to be getting younger every day. There's nice hot porridge for all of you at the mission." While she spoke, Rosie woke the children and led them out.

As Rosie was about to leave the room, she said in a timid voice, "Please, Sister, don't forget to lock the door."

Maria watched the girls as they walked away.

*Dear Lord, we are desperate for sleeping quarters for these kids.* She realised that the government's Social Services Department was unable to help.

The dark, thin, menacing shadow watched and listened and waited for the right moment.

Sister Maria looked for the boys. They weren't in their usual spot, so she climbed the stairs and walked along the platform. Here, all platforms stretched side by side like long snakes with large mouths that hissed, producing fast trains that slithered and groaned to a stop.

She found the boys tucked in a storeroom. The door had been left ajar for them. "Hello, Jacky," she said to the gangly, red-headed, Aboriginal youth.

He nodded and pushed his three younger charges out the door.

"Are ya comin', Sister?" he asked over his shoulder.

"Yes, in a moment. Go ahead. I'll catch up. I want to check on Mavis first," she said as she shooed them in the direction of the stairs. The man in the shadows watched.

She spoke to old Mavis, who sat upright on a bench while she slept. Mavis kept a newspaper open on her knees to fool those who passed, to make them think she was awake. This was her safety measure.

A loudspeaker boomed, “All passengers leave the platforms immediately. This is a terrorist alert. You must leave the station immediately.”

Trains pulled up at every platform, and passengers rushed up the stairs and escalators and into lifts. A siren was heard. The people started to panic and push as the exits became congested. People jumped off the platforms and ran along the tracks and out of the station to freedom. Some fell and twisted or broke their legs.

***All passengers leave the platforms immediately. This is a terrorist alert. You must leave the station immediately.***

The loudspeaker continued to boom. “Everyone move out of the railway station immediately; this is a terrorist alert.”

The boys were halfway up the stairs when the announcement was made. People pushed against them, and those in front started to fall. They, in turn, were pushed down, and the crowd started to step on top of and over their bodies.

“Get off, would ya!” screamed Jacky, who shielded the younger boys with his body. “See this?” he said as he flung his fist in the air and accidentally struck two rotund ladies. “Yeah, ya want some more, I’ll give it to ya. Come on, keep pushin’ and see what ya get!” he yelled. The crowd moved around the boys.

Sister Maria stood by Mavis, shocked. “Come on, old girl, I’ll help you.”

The man in the shadows moved forward, and an explosive echo was heard as a gun went off. Sister Maria fell to the ground, and the man ran in the opposite direction from the crowd.

There was silence, and all froze for a moment like a flock of birds before flight. Then, mass panic took over. The crowd stampeded up the stairs. The boys huddled together hard against the stair wall. They watched as people squashed into overcrowded lifts that jammed and stopped, leaving them suspended between two floors. Desperate screams were heard throughout the station.

Sister Maria lay on the floor in a pool of blood. She was unconscious, but she could hear the screams deep within the recesses of her mind. She cried out, but no one heard, as no sound came from her lips. She lay helpless as hell broke loose that morning at Kings Cross Railway Station.

Black helicopters could be seen in the distance. As they approached, men in black uniforms slid down ropes and ran with guns in hand.

"Stand still! Stand still, or you'll be shot!" they yelled at the people who had jumped off the platform in a bid to escape.

They stopped—all but one. A shot rang out, and the man who had lurked in the shadows now received what he was paid to give. He was killed instantly, and his blood splattered on the platform walls. He fell to the ground and lay in a pool of blood.

Terror struck the crowd. They stood silent except for a low curse here and there. They couldn't comprehend what had happened.

The disoriented crowd finally dispersed under the instructions of the United Nations Terrorist Task Force. Those who stayed behind to help the injured could hear mass sirens from ambulances that came from all directions.

Soon the Sydney Hospital's emergency department was overcrowded with patients in beds, others on stretchers, and many more left to sit and wait in the reception rooms. Many of the injured went straight to other hospitals. It seemed as if the public hospital sector in Sydney had become a war zone.

* * *

Sister Maria was resting in bed when Julie visited. They talked for some time. The guard had stepped out of the room to give Sister Maria privacy.

Sister Maria leaned forward and spoke in a whisper. "Julie, I must tell you something while the police guard isn't present. It's extremely important. Sister Teresa at St Mary's Convent told me a deadly secret."

She repeated the important secret to Julie, who sat horrified. "Please don't repeat it to anyone," she begged in a whisper, and she lay back in pain against the pillows. She thought for a moment and then added, "But you must warn the others in our class."

Julie headed to the car park. Looking up, she saw Janet and Pat walking towards her. "I am so glad to see you. I have some very important news to tell you. Sister Maria wants us to be very careful when we speak of it. Let's go and sit on that bench under the tree over there," she said, pointing. "It should be safe, as no one is about."

When sitting, Julie whispered as she leaned forward. She continued, "Father Frank is a Jesuit. His job is to report what other churches are doing, and they do this through us. We tell them unwittingly in our verbatim about our church outreach programs and also through the things we talk about in our breaks. They want to know how far their dogmas have infiltrated our churches. They want a One World Church, you know."

"That can't be," Janet wailed. "My husband says it's a lot of nonsense."

"Well, Sister Maria's friend, Sister Theresa, overheard a secret initiation into the Jesuit order and about their future plans. The information will be rewarded with death if they find out," Julie whispered. She leaned right down and spoke in a very low voice. "You know, it's not Father Frank who's been spying on us; it's Len. He's an undercover Jesuit, and it was his initiation that was overheard."

***Father Frank is a Jesuit. His job is to report what other churches are doing, and they do this through us.***

All heads jolted upright, and a look of sheer terror came across everyone's faces.

The newsreader announced: "Today we have witnessed a terrible tragedy. At Sydney Kings Cross Railway Station, a crowd was told there was a terrorist alert. This caused mass panic and a stampede, with more than twenty people injured and one person dead."

The news reader continued to read and show footage of the events. "Today, a nun's body was found face down, caught in branches in the Magdala Creek. She lived and worked at St. Mary's Convent in Springwood. Sister Theresa was shot in the head. A police investigation into her death will be organised. It has been said she was a friend of Sister Maria, who was also shot yesterday. This is Max Hiller from Australia Broadcasting Live."

## Chapter 10

# Protest Group

"Are you ready, Eddy?" Pat called. "We need to hurry if we're going to be on time for the doctor. It takes ages by train, you know!" she added as she locked the house.

Eddy, an elderly, dark-haired man with a moustache, had an easy-going, laid-back nature. He headed to the car dressed in old paint-spattered trousers and an old raggedy jumper. On his feet he wore woolly socks that were stretched and baggy and old shoes. His face wore a three-day growth.

"I don't think so, mate," she said, noticing his clothes. "You can't go to the city like that, and what's more, you'll freeze."

"Oh, did you expect me to come as well?" he answered, surprised. "I'll be fine like this, don't worry," he said after a quick inspection of himself. "You don't want to be late." Then he noticed Pat's exasperated expression, so he retreated to the bedroom and hurriedly shaved and changed into tidy clothes.

*Men!* Pat thought. *It's a pity he doesn't make an effort to wear his hearing aid; it would make life much easier for me.*

It was a bleak morning, and at the Hornsby railway station, high school and private college students shivered in the cold. Most wore extra coats or parkas over their uniforms. They stood, stamped their feet, blew steam from their mouths, clapped, and shook their gloved hands as they talked and laughed. The men who regularly commuted wore black coats over their suits, and the women had long coats over slacks or skirts, with boots, and wore warm gloves and long scarves, and some wore beanies on their heads. They stood quiet and solemn as they contemplated what their day held for them, and occasionally, stamped their feet to keep warm. Some of the men read morning newspapers.

When Pat and Eddy reached the station, they had to run to catch the train. Once onboard, Eddy watched houses flash by.

"Eddy, look at all those houses on the market. I wonder if we should put our place on the market and go further out." She looked at him and tapped his arm. "Did you hear what I said, Eddy? We should sell our house, with all the trade laws now in place, and move away from the suburbs."

"What for?" Eddy asked, shocked. "We own our property and have a big garden. We have fruit trees, plenty of water, and no close neighbours. We should be fine."

Pat continued. "We should move into an isolated place," she explained, but Eddy didn't respond. He stubbornly looked out the window.

Pat also looked out the window. She watched people attending their daily business and noticed houses up for sale and others repossessed. Many were empty and had unkempt yards, littered with junk mail blown over weeds and caught in bushes.

She thought about problems broadcast on TV. *The experts spoke about the recession worsening into a depression and the real-estate market dropping, making original loans higher than equity in properties and repayments impossible to maintain, forcing people out of their homes.* She thought about the increase in food prices. *It's strange how we all dismiss things we hear and see and try to continue with business as usual. It's like we all live in a vacuum. Perhaps it's because we can't do anything about it, so we just put it aside. I certainly don't know what goes on in Eddy's mind.*

When they arrived in the city, they spent about two hours in the doctor's room and the rest of the day on business and in shops. In the park they met their daughter, Roslyn, and her two small sons, Jason and France.

"Hello, boys," Pat said, as she stooped down with a kiss for each of her grandsons, which they duly wiped from their faces. "What lovely thick coats and caps—and look at your new boots! Aren't they great!" she said as she patted their heads.

"Tell Grandpa what you have in your hands," Roslyn said. "Come on; Grandpa would love to see."

As they settled on a seat, the boys proudly produced their latest iPads with the games they were playing. Eddy placed the youngest boy on his knee so he could get a better look.

"You two look lovely and warm," Roslyn commented to her parents. She leaned over to feel their new cardigans. "Mum, are these the cardigans you've been knitting?"

"Yes, the cable stitch was quite complicated, but I finished in time for this cold spell," said Pat, nodding.

"Dad, please be careful when you go back to the railway station. The schools are allowing children right across Australia to have a free day, so they can march in a rally for climate change. They intend to march through the city to Government House. It could get out of hand. It's been on the news all day."

"Well! I have heard everything now," responded Eddy. "Children telling the government what to do. Thanks, we will take care." He hugged his daughter goodbye.

They were nearly at the railway station at Circular Quay when a large crowd of children, parents, and youth marched past with banners. They yelled for changes to be made and jostled against each other. The crowd came from all directions as they marched and protested against the lack of commitment by the government toward climate change issues. Eddy and Pat found themselves being pushed along with the group. Pat grabbed Eddy's hand as he was jostled ahead of her. He stepped aside and pulled Pat back, against a wall, out of the main thrust of the crowd.

Eddy grabbed her arm and pulled her into a door that had just been opened by an old lady peeping out. "Please, can we stay here until they pass?" he asked breathlessly. "We were caught in the crowd and dragged along."

She looked at Pat, who was pale with shock. "Of course," she said.

The room they were ushered into had old lounge chairs at one end and two long tables and chairs in the middle. Against one wall was a sink with a tea urn. At the other end were doors to male and female toilets. *We must be at the back of an office block or shops,* Pat thought.

The old lady looked out of the window, and Pat and Eddy joined her. The crowd stopped when the police arrived in their vans. Some police assembled along the edge of the street. Others busily taped off the street or placed wooden barricades that blocked many from going forward, but from the side streets, people kept pushing and emerged further along. Soon the marches came to Government House and waited for a response from a government delegate.

The police assembled in front of Government House. A voice came over a loudspeaker. "Please, all go home. Do you hear me? It is time now to finish your protest. It has been a peaceful protest, and we thank you for this. Go home and watch yourselves on the news tonight." The officer demanded.

That evening, the TV stations filmed and recorded what had happened in Australia that day. The announcers showed footage of the protest not only in Sydney but in all the other major cities of Australia, as well as throughout the world.

# Chapter 11

# Nuclear Power Stations

The next morning, a squadron of black helicopters filled the sky like a swarm of locusts about to strike. They patrolled over the nuclear power stations twenty kilometres inland from Goulburn, southwest of Sydney, then flew to Sydney.

The Australian Government had recently erected four nuclear power stations. These were in Goulburn and in the mountains behind Brisbane, Adelaide, and Melbourne. This was a new world trend since other fuel was nearly impossible to obtain now, and global warming was a world issue.

"What do you think would happen if terrorists bombed one of these places?" Brad's co-pilot, Ross, asked.

"Well, mate, I hate to think. They're far enough from the cities, so the direct blast wouldn't affect the people there, but the fallout would certainly upset things for any town closer," he reasoned. "Mate, I don't know what we'd do without the surveillance equipment we have in these machines. It's great; we can see satellite images inside buildings and even in cars—and we can run car number plates through these computers and get all the data about their owners within moments. Have you used this equipment?"

"No, not yet," Ross replied.

* * *

"Janet, quick, come here! Just have a look at this!" Albert yelled.

Janet ran outside to see a squadron of black helicopters in the distance. As they approached and passed, they covered the sky like a swarm of locusts, with rotors that whirled and roared like mighty warriors.

"Brad is on duty today!" Janet yelled back against the noise.

Albert cupped his ear but couldn't hear what she said. He shook his head and shrugged.

Eighteen-year-old Anita, barefoot and in pyjamas, appeared at the door.

"Did you say my famous big brother was on duty?" She laughed with excitement.

"Yes, it's probably him now in one of those choppers!" Janet yelled back.

"Terrorists, look out; you're in trouble now!" Anita shouted to the sky.

* * *

"Look! There's my folks' place down there," Brad said, pointing as they flew over the last mountain ridge.

"This computer technology is really awesome," he continued. "The United Nations is going to issue a biometrical-coded ID card that can identify fingerprints, retinal scans, and DNA of every person in the world. When they do, they'll have all our information, and it'll be used in place of money and bankcards. Believe me, it'll be much easier to trace crime once that's in place. We'll be able to access all the information through these little computers here on these choppers."

***The United Nations is going to issue a biometrical-coded ID card that can identify fingerprints, retinal scans, and DNA of every person in the world.***

"I see," Ross said, not really impressed. "Don't we have a group to check in the city?"

"Sure do, mate; we're heading there now."

* * *

Janet and Anita came into the kitchen to find Albert with the TV blaring while he read the morning paper.

"We're leaving, dear," Janet said, and as she passed, she patted him on the shoulder. "Anita and I are going to the city this morning. Don't forget we all must be home by six so we can be ready for my graduation. I'll have my phone with me if you need to call, dear."

Albert grunted but didn't look up.

"Goodbye, Dad," Anita said and kissed the top of his bald head as she passed.

In the car, Anita asked her mother why she hadn't mentioned the meeting they were attending that morning.

"I didn't want to upset your father. You know how he is with religion." But to herself, she thought: *There's been something different about Albert lately.*

# Chapter 12
# City Meeting

Janet and Anita knocked on the back door of the department store on George Street. Sister Maria opened it, and a voice greeted them from inside.

"Come in, you two!" Julie called. "I've been waiting for you. Come and sit here," she said with a big grin.

They entered a room where tables had been pushed together, and chairs and couches were filled with smiling people. There were Julie and Jacky, the boy from the mission, and three Catholic nuns who were friends of Sister Maria.

Sister Maria stood by the door. She looked pale from her ordeal at the railway station. There was a large dressing around her upper right arm where she had been shot. "I would like you to meet Anna," she said. "She's the caretaker and cleaner of this staff room and has permission to use this room as long as we meet after hours."

Anna was an elderly, thin lady who stood with a stoop. Her deeply-wrinkled face framed bright blue eyes that noticed every word and action. She was a Christian Jew whose parents had witnessed and escaped the terrible Holocaust during the Second World War.

She spoke up. "I met your friends Eddy and Pat the day school children and their families marched to Government House to protest against planet-warming issues." Her voice was strong, with no accent, which surprised Janet.

"Yes, they told me about it," Janet answered in a timid voice.

"We're all here now, so let's kneel and pray so that we can start our study," Sister Maria requested.

Chairs were pushed back, and all nine people present in that small room knelt in prayer.

Sister Maria spoke to the little group. "We learnt in our last meeting that in Emperor Nero's time, the Jews became unpopular in the empire, primarily because of their resurgent nationalistic feelings. This caused an explosion of violence against them almost everywhere.

"The early Christians, of whom some were Jews, but many more were Gentiles, kept the Sabbath. These poor people were tortured in the cruellest fashion. They were placed in Roman coliseums, fighting lions and gladiators for the thrill of the Roman crowd.

"At that time, the heathen nations infiltrated the Roman Empire with 'Sun worship.' Emperor Constantine decided to unite both religions to bring about peace. By the fifth century, the Roman Catholic Church had assumed not only religious but political power and Sunday became firmly rooted as the day of worship in Christianity. Our Catholic Church has claimed credit for the transfer from Saturday to Sunday, and in the past, used its inquisitional powers against dissenters of the church.

"We know from our church history that General Berthier in 1798 overthrew the pope and placed him in prison. From that point the pope didn't have the same powers as he had in the past."

"We see in Revelation 13:11," another nun answered, "a lamblike beast that spoke as a dragon. When we study Bible history, we realise the only power that came into play about that time, with lamblike tendencies toward religious freedom and liberties, was the United States. It drew up a new constitution known as the Bill of Rights. We read this lamblike power will speak with the voice of a dragon. The voice of a dragon is the voice of religious intolerance and persecution."

Sister Maria read on. "In verse 12, it says, 'and he will exercise all the power of the first beast before him, and cause the earth and them which dwell therein to worship the first beast, whose deadly wound was healed.'" She looked around the group. "We know this is the papacy that had the deadly wound."

"So, America will make her constitution void," Julie exclaimed, shocked.

Sister Maria explained. "America will set up laws against freedom of worship. The nation will deny all dissenters the privilege to buy and sell and will persecute these people, and believe me, Australia will follow as will the rest of the world."

Sister Maria continued. "We have studied in the Bible God's ten commandments and have come to realise that it's important to keep the right day. As nuns, we were taught that our pope is God's vicar on earth and has the power to change the day. We realise now this isn't true. Revelation 14, verse 12, tells us God's people will be commandment-keeping people, with the faith of Jesus."

Their Bibles were still open when a helicopter was heard passing overhead. Everyone stopped, looked up, and listened.

"Brad told me that the choppers have satellite equipment that can see us in rooms like in this building. I wonder if it's Brad above us now," said Anita.

"Shivers," Jacky squealed, "they ain't gonna see me in 'ere." He rushed out the door and down the side street, knocking over bins. He pushed past kids on bikes and out into the traffic. Horns blasted as cars narrowly missed him. The chopper followed. Then there it was: a police car, with two cops standing by the doors with hands on the pistols in their holsters.

"Well, what do we have here?" Albert asked. "It looks to me like trouble. Gutter trouble by the looks of him." He grabbed Jacky and pushed his arm hard up his back, so hard that Jacky stood on tiptoe to avoid the pain. His face was pushed into the bonnet of the cop car while his arm was forced still higher.

"Oh, shivers! Ya breakin' me arm!" Jacky yelled. They frisked him, ignoring his cries.

"He's clean; let's take him to the lockup for the night. That should make him think twice. He might decide to tell us why he ran when he saw the chopper," Albert said.

They drove west on the Great Western Highway from Sydney and soon were at Chatsworth Police Station.

After they completed the necessary paperwork, Albert mumbled, "Throw him in the holding cell. I dare say Sister Maria will collect him later."

## Chapter 13

# Graduation

Eddy sat in his lounge room, watching the news on TV while he waited for Pat to get ready.

The reporter announced. "The Australian Government has in place programs that will advise and educate the public on global greenhouse gas emissions caused by our lifestyle. The government will continue to provide funds for solar energy and water-efficient products. This is Max Hiller from Australia Broadcasting Live News."

"Well, I'm ready," Pat said, as she stood in front of Eddy in her new dress, waiting expectantly for a comment. Eddy stood and headed to the kitchen. *He didn't even notice,* Pat thought, disappointed.

"Eddy, look at my new dress." Eddy turned and looked but didn't comment. "Well, does it look okay?" she asked.

"I will tell you if it doesn't, so why do you ask?" mumbled Eddy, who never took notice of fashion.

They drove to the meeting in silence. Pat rebuked herself for feeling disappointed with Eddy's lack of response. *Yes*, she thought, *I must keep my eyes on Jesus and think about how I can help others*. She thought about her morning at the hospital and the struggle others faced with life-threatening illnesses.

Pat and Eddy entered the main hall. A buzz of conversation echoed off the walls around them in a dull roar, making individual words impossible to determine. Acoustics, it seemed, had not been a prime consideration for whoever designed this room; Eddy found the noise uncomfortable as he already had poor hearing.

The hall was crowded with suited grey-haired men and women in formal attire. Pat saw Julie and her family enter the hall. Julie's long blond hair curved around her chin, framing laughing blue eyes and a dimpled smile. She wore a black dress that floated a few centimetres above her knees.

Julie's family were given drinks and offered nibbles. The children were thrilled to have their soft drinks served in adult champagne glasses. Julie laughed at their excited faces.

Julie looked across the hall and waved to her friends. As she approached, she spoke with excitement. "Well, look at you two! You look lovely, Pat. Soft blue is certainly your colour. It suits you so well—and look at you, Janet, in your smart black slacks."

Quickly, they introduced their families. Anita and her friend, Tommy, plus Brad and Albert, stood together and nodded and shook hands as they were introduced to the others. Pat and Eddy's daughter and grandchildren were away in the country. Julie's husband, Robert, shook Albert's hand and noticed the strength in his grip. He especially noticed Albert's rugged dark features, thick eyebrows, and robust body.

Sometime later, Father Frank, with his sober manner and sour expression, stood and announced it was time to go into the main lecture hall. As they entered, Sister Maria came on stage and sang a sweet melody. All were surprised and thrilled when they heard their friend sing. As she sang, families were shown their seats, and the fifty graduating students were escorted to the two front rows. They were excited and also very relieved that their studies were over, and now, they were about to graduate.

Father Frank was the emcee for the evening. He spoke about the six-monthly programs and projected on the wall photos of activities and events. As the three friends watched, they noticed the other groups had a pleasant time in their classes. There were many snaps of them laughing and discussing their verbatim together. Nothing like that had ever happened in Father Frank's classes.

When their class was called up, Sister Maria was first to receive her certificate, then Janet, Pat, and Julie gratefully received theirs. Len took his with a knowing smirk.

Julie leaned toward Pat as she followed her down the steps and off the platform.

"I wonder if they'll make Len graduate every year," she whispered.

Pat giggled and turned, placing her hand across her mouth. "I dare say they will, so he can spy for them."

When all was complete, a choir came on stage and sang in perfect harmony, transporting them into a realm of beauty. It was a fitting end to a pleasant evening.

# Chapter 14

# City

"Mum, I'm off," Anita called. "Brad, on his way to work, is going to take me to the City Mission. I'll meet Tommy after at Central Railway Station and go home with him, but we'll come back in time to watch the program on global warming."

Janet came into the hall. "Please be very careful, Anita, it's so dangerous these days for a young girl to be on her own, especially in the city."

*When you leave the mission, get a cab or a lift with somebody. I didn't want to worry Mum, but lately, it's getting out of hand. The whole world's gone mad.*

Brad entered the hall and answered his mother's concerns. "Don't worry, Mum. It's only a short walk to the station. Oh! By the way, you do realise, Dad's at work tonight?"

"Yes, he told me. Take care of yourself while at work, won't you, Brad?" And then, "Bye-bye, Anita!" she called.

When in the car, Brad warned his sister. "Sis, Mum's right—it's very dangerous, I can tell you, so when you leave the mission, get a cab or a lift with somebody. I didn't want to worry Mum, but lately, it's getting out of hand. The whole world's gone mad. Now, promise me you'll find a lift."

"Yes, yes, stop fussing. I hear what you say."

* * *

Anita stood silently, preparing soup vegetables with the other helpers at Sister Maria's. A helicopter could be heard in the distance, and she wondered if it was Brad on his city patrol. She remembered his warning.

"June, can I get a lift later with you, please?"

June nodded and smiled. "Sure thing."

When in the car, June remembered she had another appointment and had to stay on the highway. "I'll pull in here, at this bus stop. If you go across the road and down through that block of shops, you should be near the station," she explained to Anita.

Anita headed off, but after a short while, she realised she was lost. She pulled out her mobile phone and called Tommy, hoping he could give her instructions on where to go, or even better still, come and get her. The LED screen lit up, informing her there was no signal. She hurried down a side street, hoping it would lead her to Central Railway Station.

A police car came silently from nowhere and pulled up across from her. An officer jumped out and grabbed a young woman standing by the side of the road and sped off, tyres screeching. Shouts broke out, and a scruffy young man next to Anita pulled out a gun and fired at the disappearing car. The sound of the shots exploded in her head, and her ears hurt. She stood there petrified, too scared to move. She was amazed that he was so close and didn't seem to notice her.

A small child ran out of a tenement block onto the street and screamed for her mother. The scruffy man lowered his weapon and watched, then turned and disappeared. A neighbour rushed from the building, grabbed the child, and ducked back in, and the door slammed behind them.

Anita, her heart racing, quickly walked on. The street she was in led to an alley behind a main shopping centre. She walked past rubbish-filled wheelie bins and nearly tripped over a drugged, homeless man who lay in a pool of vomit. She jumped back, wondering what to do. She decided she could do nothing. Just move, she told herself, get out of here as quickly as you can.

Further on, she met a drunken old lady with a supermarket trolley, scratching through the rubbish in a wheelie bin. She was hungry, no doubt. Anita stopped and gave her all her change, which wasn't much. The lady was bleary-eyed and dirty, with whiskers on her heavily wrinkled face. She smiled a toothless smile and hobbled away, pushing her trolley.

Anita turned the corner and hurried up the main street, hopefully toward the railway station. The shops were closed because it was Sunday. As she approached the corner, she noticed three girls about twelve to thirteen years old standing together, waiting for their bus. They were nicely dressed. *Perhaps they just came from church*, she thought.

Suddenly, two cars sped up to where they stood, and men jumped out, grabbing the girls. They screamed for help. Anita looked around, but people walked on as if they didn't see or hear a thing. *Robotic people with no heart*, she thought as she shrank back into the doorway of a closed shop.

She grabbed her mobile with trembling hands. She shook so much she could hardly hit the triple-0 emergency number.

"Police, ambulance, or fire?"

"The police; hurry, please," Anita whispered.

A few moments later, a voice spoke. "Sergeant James speaking."

Anita looked up at the street sign. "I'm on George Street," she looked around, "and I'm standing in front of Toni's Barber Shop. Three girls were abducted ... Yes, they were of fair complexion ... The cars—well, one was old and blue and the other white, I think ... Number plates—I don't know ... Please, just hurry ... They went in the direction of the Harbour Bridge."

She stood and listened to a chopper circle overhead and watched it fly toward the Harbour Bridge. She realised she was still lost and now, very much afraid.

She silently prayed as tears crept down her cheeks. "Lord, I'm so tired of this wicked world. How can people be so bad? Please, Lord, I'm so tired of it all. Your angels must weep at the sights they endure down here. Please, come soon and end this wickedness."

As she finished her whispered prayer a man approached. He bent his elbow for her to link her arm in his.

He spoke softly. "Come, I will show you the way to the station." He was a short, rotund man, with a round, gentle face which smiled kindly at her.

She took his arm. It was a very dangerous thing to do, but how did he know where she wanted to go? Perhaps he was her guardian angel. She wondered why she thought such a thing. After what she had just witnessed, she was surprised she felt perfectly happy to let him guide her. They walked along the footpath. He stopped and waited for the road to clear.

"Watch your step; the streets are dirty down here," he gently said and smiled, more to himself than to her.

Anita swung her head and noticed his expression. She thought to herself, *What an angelic thing to say.* She didn't think the streets were any worse than usual: there were papers and an odd syringe here and there, but she supposed it would look filthy to someone from a better place, and he did say "down here."

When on the other side of the street, he stopped and pointed. She could see the station entrance clearly. She turned to thank him, but he was gone.

Tommy came out of the station; he was worried about Anita. The roar of a chopper filled the air, and he lifted his head and watched it weave between the high-rise buildings. It was obviously chasing someone. Suddenly, two cars came screeching around the corner and sped past. There were girls in the car, screaming and fighting with male occupants. His heart sank, and he started to panic. *Oh! Lord, please, not Anita; don't let one of those girls be Anita*, he prayed.

The next moment, Anita rushed into Tommy's arms, glad to see him. "Those men—I saw them grab those girls, and I rang the police. I'm so glad the police moved quickly," Anita explained. She was shaking all over and now started to cry quietly.

Tommy held her tightly as he looked over her shoulder at another scene. She turned to see cops drag off an evil-looking man who was spitting at people nearby. He curled his lips in a sneer that displayed black, broken teeth. He did single finger signs and laughed at staring people.

***It was all too much. Anita collapsed into Tommy's arms, sobbing deeply. How could one be calm in a world like this?***

"He's that serial killer the newspapers warned us about," Tommy said with a shudder. "I'm glad he's caught at long last."

It was all too much. Anita collapsed into Tommy's arms, sobbing deeply. How could one be calm in a world like this?

They sat silently in the moving train. Tommy held Anita as she cried. Choppers thudded above, manoeuvring between high-rise buildings. They were seen more and more in the city because of the overwhelming increase in crime.

## Chapter 15

# Planet Warming

Sunday evening, ten-year-old Beth called to her mother. “Mummy, can I watch the global warming program instead of going to bed?”

“Do you think you’ll understand the program, dear?” Julie asked.

“We’re studying it at school, and my teacher told us not to miss it, as she wants to discuss in class what we saw,” Beth explained.

“Well, you’d better get your jobs finished, so you don’t miss it,” Julie suggested.

Family worship was over. John was tucked into bed, and Robert turned on the TV to Australia Broadcasting Live just as the Sunday program started.

A reporter spoke: “In a frozen corner of the United States, an arctic crisis has unfolded. An Alaskan island no longer exists. Its people have been forced to abandon their homes because of the pace of global warming. A few years ago, when American scientists raised the alarm, they were obstructed.”

“I have with me here a leading scientist. Mr. Uzenni, how did the American government obstruct your reports?”

The scientist looked directly into the camera. “They would take our reports and alter them in such a way as to systematically play down the global warming problem.”

The reporter faced the scientist and spoke. “It’s in the Arctic that the tragedy facing the earth is most powerfully evident. Here, amidst the spectacle of huge ice melt, international scientists compiled a startling report to warn what it means to humanity in this century. You described the seas as rising and coasts under threat with an increase in hurricanes that will bring huge devastation. You say the sea will rise about one metre, and many islands will not exist.”

Mr. Uzenni agreed. “Yes, but our recommendation was kept from America’s public due to the election, and still they haven’t been told all the truth, even though it has been several years since the last election, and a new election is on the horizon.”

The reporter shuffled his papers. "Your key message was for governments to cut greenhouse gas emissions urgently. When the president heard this, his government stepped in. What did they do?"

"The scientists were asked to delay work on their policy recommendations. The government argued that the preparation of the report had a fundamental flaw. They wanted its authors to stick to the science. This was seen by scientists as a delaying tactic."

The reporter butted in. "And a year later, the report was finally ready for publication. Its publication was delayed until after the nation voted and was changed so much that it made all that was said non-effective."

"That's right," nodded Mr. Uzenni. "The strongest evidence in the report stated that humans are affecting the earth's climate system. After I presented that evidence in a speech, a number of individuals from the private sector came up to me and said they thought the speech was too strong, and they never wanted to hear it again."

The reporter looked grave but continued. "The president formally rejected the process in which the world was uniting to cut emissions. He opposed these groups before he became president and continues to oppose them. His reasons are the same today as they were before. His cabinet had and has close ties to industry."

"The vice president runs an oil service company. His commerce chief owns an oil company. The chairman of a giant manufacturing company runs the president's treasury. His chief of staff is a senior car industry lobbyist. They have agreed that it's bad for their economy, and if it's bad for us, we're not going to do it; this is their slogan. It tends to be a form of boot-in-your-face government. It's 'we have the power, we have the money, we have the votes, and we're not interested in talking to you with your reform ideas. We have our agenda to run.'"

"The world is changing dramatically," added Mr. Uzenni. "For the last five years, we have recorded the hottest years on record. Each year is getting hotter and dryer and storms are more frequent. We're getting very close to the tipping point, with climates out of control."

He continued. "Scientists say if action is not taken within the next five years, millions of the world poorest could face drought and starvation. Heat and ice-melt will swell seas far more than originally predicted, and this means mainland America will be affected, too. For the last five to ten years, the public has not been fully informed, and we have not taken the initial steps that need to be taken. If we continue on this path for another five years, we're going to be at the point of no return. We may be there now—who knows?" The reporter smiled grimly as the lights faded.

Robert stretched and said to Julie, "I bet next month, at election time, they'll have a change in government. It's certainly needed, and our prime minister has started a few programs to lessen its effects, but much more is needed at this late date."

"Look who didn't stay awake? I wonder how much she saw," Julie laughed.

Robert picked up Beth and carried her to her room.

Julie switched to another TV station to get the late news. It was filming China and its citizens. Well-dressed people walked briskly along the busy thoroughfare about their business. The 5G cameras mounted on light poles filmed the actions of these citizens. One could see them walking and then falling flat on their faces, dead.

Julie called to Robert. "Quick, come and see what's happening on the news. Robert, be quick! You will miss it." Robert raced back to the lounge room and sat next to Julie.

The reporter announced excitedly. "China's citizens are being attacked by a new deadly flu- virus. The virus is different from all others in the past. It is believed to have leaked out of a government experimental research laboratory. The leading scientist contacted the authorities, but when a further investigation was made, he was found dead, and the cause isn't known."

Now the cameras went to an Australian citizen living and working in China. They showed his recorded footage as he spoke into the phone. "Police are knocking on the doors of citizens' homes here in China. Look, they are dragging them out. The citizens are kicking and lying down, screaming. Several police have joined the attack, dragging them to police vans. Other citizens are running as fast as they can down the street. Some are dropping dead in front of us. It is terrible. The disease is spreading quickly. The old are worse affected and are dying where they stand. I believe the hospitals are already full of the dying, and tent hospitals are being erected in the parks."

The news reporter came back onto the screen. "The governments of the world need to act quickly as this virus will take over the world, killing millions. All overseas travel must be cancelled, and those coming home to Australia from different countries are to be quarantined for two weeks in a designated motel. But how and what does one look for with this new virus," he announced soberly.

## Chapter 16

# Terrorist Task Force

Jacky sat in his cell. He was next to the office and could see and hear all that transpired. He felt he was part of the action. He sat back and listened. It was Sunday morning, and the police officers from the special Terrorist Task Force unit had been brought in. They were on a special mission.

Many voices were raised and urgent as they entered the station. Albert pulled down a map on his office wall with nearby districts. "These are Islamic homes, and it's important to bring these men in for interrogation. They're suspects in local terrorist movements," he explained. "I want you to go in twos. Make sure you bring them back."

"Sergeant," said one of the cops, "what if they're not there? Will we go back later?"

"Sure, sure, that's the idea. We'll all assemble here after the raid and report. If they're not at home, we'll organise another raid later. We'll hold them for questioning until Monday, when the special interrogation team arrives," Albert answered.

The map was examined, and districts were divided, and soon, the men were organised. Brad and Ross went together.

"We have the Rockdale area," Brad said. "Remember, we saw suspicious activity in the warehouses at Rockdale when on chopper duty. We'll check it out after this job."

"Maybe we'll expose some drug dealers, if not terrorists. It's near Sydney Airport—who would know?" Ross remarked. He was young and inexperienced.

After some time, Brad spoke. "We're at Sunshine Avenue; it's an old area, isn't it? Here we go, number 178, a green weatherboard. Let's go," he said as he switched off the vehicle.

It was Sunday morning, and nobody seemed to be around. Brad and Ross walked up the path and noisily knocked on the front door, but no one answered. They stepped aside and caught sight of a broken front window.

"It looks like a break-in," Ross said. "Look at the couch—it's been torn, and there's foam padding everywhere."

Brad stepped through the broken window and opened the front door. The room was a mess with the TV face down on the floor. The couch had been cut several times, and its stuffing was scattered across the room. Dishes and vases were broken, and fragments were scattered over the floor.

"Man! There's been an almighty struggle here. It looks like the intruders were after something in this couch," Brad said as he ran his hand inside the lining.

Suddenly, a woman appeared at the door. "I noticed your police car," she said. "I'm glad you're here. Last night, at midnight, a black Mercedes sedan pulled up in front of my house. I didn't see anybody go into Kamisem's home, but I heard them. They smashed that window, and all hell broke loose. What a terrible noise; I was scared stiff. I rang the police, but they didn't come." She stared at the destruction. "They're such a quiet family. No trouble at all." She shook her head. "Their two-year-old screamed and screamed. He would have been woken by the noise." Then, as a second thought: "I saw four men push the family into the Mercedes and drive away. They were dressed in long white coats or something. Very strange, if you ask me." She clucked her tongue.

***What was going on? Who had removed these families, and to where, and why?***

When the police units returned and reported to headquarters, they all had the same story. All twenty homes were wrecked and empty. The men wanted for questioning had violently disappeared into thin air.

What was going on? Who had removed these families, and to where, and why?

* * *

That evening, Robert was on a short shift from 10:00 p.m. to 2:00 a.m., filling in for a nurse who had called in sick. He was amazed at the number of Islamic people coming in after accidents or street fights. *Things are getting worse and worse,* he thought. He was glad to complete his charts and head home.

*No! I'm nearly out of fuel. I must pull into the next fuel station. Well, here's one, and I'm the only one here; that's good*, he thought.

Exhausted, he walked back to his car when he noticed at the traffic lights several cars with Ku Klux Klan members. Robert jumped into his car, managed to get the lights, and followed a few cars behind. They travelled through many districts before pulling up in a leafy street. Robert swung into a side street and parked. He walked silently to the corner. Two men were whispering together. They stood under the street light. He pushed back against some bushes, hoping they wouldn't see him.

The taller of the two pulled off his headgear for just a moment to adjust it. It was long enough for Robert to recognise who it was. What a shock. It was Sergeant Albert Smith—Janet's Albert.

The other man was speaking. The man's voice was easily recognised. It was Father Frank.

Albert answered him. "If anyone rings the emergency number, it'll be transferred to my office and delayed until tomorrow. We'll deal with it in our own way then. We must be quick and get these people. I believe there are many Islamic homes we're visiting tonight."

Robert pushed himself further back into the bushes. He was shocked. *Well! I now know who's responsible for the missing Islamic families.*

# Chapter 17
# Springwood Convent

The captured Islamic families had been held at St Mary's Convent in Springwood for nearly twenty-four hours. The men were placed in holding cells in the basement, and women and children were located in the convent's rooms above.

Father Frank sipped his tea and spoke to Len. "The police have been given orders to investigate the disappearances of these people. We know it will only be a short, superficial inquiry because the government and the heads of the police department are behind all this. The demand for their evacuation came directly from them. News media are all over this story, so the cops have to make it look good."

They watched the children at play in the convent's locked courtyard. The grounds were isolated from the other homes and buildings in the Springwood district, high in the mountains behind Sydney. The voices of children at play wouldn't be heard, but all the same, they needed to get these families evacuated as soon as possible.

"Will the families be sent to their homelands?" a priest asked.

"Yes." Father Frank answered. "Most Islamic families are innocent immigrants, but we have been alarmed to find that Australian-born Islamic people have ventured overseas to train as terrorists."

"Why would people want to turn weapons of mass destruction on their own people and country?" the priest asked.

Father Frank continued. "The seemingly innocent white-clad Muslim youth of today can easily become the home-grown jihadist of tomorrow. They pose a real threat to Australia, which has fed, clothed, sheltered, and educated them. Government efforts to keep terrorists out are made with a degree of futility because the sad truth is, the terrorist is already here and part of Australia's society. Today, it is a common practice by extremist groups to radicalise their children by watching jihadist videos online. Also, the U.S. and British counter-terrorism officials said the variety of foreign fighters from all nations, streaming into Syria, is unprecedented in recent history."

"They are going to Syria regardless and will not be allowed back. They will have to make do with their new country."

"When will they fly the families out?" the priest asked.

Father Frank turned to look at both men.

Albert continued with the conversation. "We can't be too careful. If they stay too long, someone might hear or see the children, and this mustn't happen, no matter what. They'll be removed at midnight and taken to the army's private airport. On arrival, they'll immediately be flown out. Syria can do whatever they want with them when they get there."

The priest nodded and reminded them of the current situation. "Because of the virus outbreak in Australia, there has been a national travel ban. Both ways, in and out. But I suppose they will be going out of the country, so, at least, that won't affect Australia with their corona pandemic over there, which I believe is at horrendous proportions."

Father Frank speaks in guarded manner. "The Australian citizens will not agree with any of this, so we will need our disguises." As a second thought. "Yes, I agree, they will have to put up with whatever when they get there."

The families were given their evacuation orders in the dining hall that evening. They were to be dressed, packed, and ready by midnight.

At exactly midnight, a covered army truck pulled up before the foyer's clock finished striking. Behind came two black cars. Eight men entered the foyer, dressed in white gowns and hoods. These men dressed as the Ku Klux Klan were the same who had violently removed these families from their homes. At the sight of the gowns and hoods, the children started to cry and whimper; some screamed in fear.

The men walked swiftly past the group, then upstairs to the second-floor balcony, and under the veranda's dark arches, they watched the evacuation.

* * *

Jacky sat on his cell floor and listened to conversations taking place in the office. It was Monday morning, and the Special Unit was there to interrogate terrorists, but instead, they told stories of how they had disappeared in the night and of sightings of Ku Klux Klan members in the area.

A new voice at the front reception area could be heard. It was Sister Maria; she had come to collect him. Jacky was glad to see her and very glad to get out of the place. In his mind he knew something very crooked had happened, but just what, he couldn't fathom.

When in the car, he shared what he had heard with Sister Maria, who listened with a worried expression. Jacky could tell she knew more than she let on. She suddenly changed the subject.

"Jacky, you should be witnessing to your friends about your faith. You know, the people of the night and others."

"I ain't bin taught books, Sister. How can I?" Jacky said in a high-pitched squeal.

"Jacky, God sends a professional person to solicitors, doctors, and bankers. He sends a person who understands life in the country to farmers; and He can send you, if you're willing, to the people of the night. You understand their ways because you have lived amongst them. Jacky, you have a good mind, and you remember what you've heard. Share with these people what you've learned in our group studies.'

***Just remember, Jacky, it's ordinary people living lives under the direction of an extraordinary God and who are doing God's work.***

Jacky looked at her, wide-eyed. "Do ya think, Sister?"

Sister Maria nodded. "Just remember, Jacky, it's ordinary people living lives under the direction of an extraordinary God and who are doing God's work. In 2 Corinthians 12:9, we are told: 'My grace is sufficient for you, for My strength is made perfect in weakness.'"

* * *

Robert sat quietly, eating his breakfast as Julie organised the children for school. When the school bus drove away, she came in and noticed his worried expression. *He's hardly slept for nights, and he just tosses and turns, so I suppose he should look haggard,* she thought.

"Darling, you should go back to bed. You look so tired," she said, sitting opposite him at the table.

"Jules, you have no idea what I saw Saturday night." He then explained what happened. "They are capturing Islamic families—why and what for, I don't know. Albert and Father Frank are disguising themselves as Ku Klux Klan members. It can't be good."

Julie was shocked. "We must warn the others, especially Janet. I'm sure she doesn't know what her husband's up to." She stood and walked toward the phone.

Robert caught her arm as she passed. "We need to think carefully before we do anything. How do you know that Janet won't tell Albert what I saw—and our phone could be bugged. Who would know? I think we should first get our family out of here, perhaps for now, to your mum's in the country. None of your friends know where she lives."

"Yes, and I think we should put the property on the market while we can," added Julie. "We've been shown in our Bible study group when the Sunday law for worship comes into effect, if we don't go along with the government and its environment issues, we will be treated as a terrorist and be imprisoned. Now that we've decided as a family to keep the Saturday Sabbath, they'll consider we're not in line with their policies, and I dare say we'll be in for it. Also, the virus is getting worse. Beth said three of her friends from school are in the hospital at the moment with the virus. I feel it's too much of a health risk to send the kids to school at the moment, so it'll be good to take them to the country, for now."

Robert started to clear the dishes. "I'll go down to the real estate agent as soon as I finish here. Ring your mum and ask her if we can spend some time at the farm. Don't say why. Tell her you'll explain when you get there. Go straight after picking up the kids from school."

Julie reached for the phone on the kitchen wall. "But what are you going to do, Robert?"

"Don't worry; I'll be right behind you. Don't think for a moment I'm staying here. I'll put the house on the market and then do my afternoon shift. I'm coming down with something, so I'll sign off sick and be out of there. I'll resign later. They owe me sick pay, lots of it, and holiday pay, too, if I'm not mistaken."

Julie tried to sound excited when she picked the children up from school. "We're going to Grandma's for a holiday. Won't that be fun?" she said.

"Hooray! We're going to Grandma's!" John shouted.

"Well, that's good timing, Mum. Today, we were told next week, all schools will be closed because of the virus. They said it has been on the news all day," explained Beth.

Still trying to sound excited but very apprehensive, Julie answered, "We are packed and leaving right now. Isn't that a great surprise?"

"No, you can't, Mum. You promised we would go after school to Susie's. You know how sick she is. Her mother said she's been asking for me. Please, Mum, you promised!" Beth wailed.

"That's right. I'm so sorry—I forgot. We'll go there right now," Julie said as she turned the car around.

When they arrived, Susie's mother, Penny, spoke to Julie in a quiet tone, so the children in the bedroom wouldn't hear.

John played on the back veranda with Buster, Susie's dog. He would have done anything to have a lovely Kelpie like Buster. He threw a ball, and Buster galloped after it.

"It's cancer," Penny explained. "They say she has only a few weeks, or perhaps a month or so. The doctors feel it's best for her to stay at home as long as she can."

Penny started to cry, and Julie held her close. She didn't have any words to say. She just held her and felt her friend's pain. She wondered how her own faith would hold if she had been told such devastating news about her own two.

Beth, on the other hand, had plenty to say. Susie had asked her what and where heaven was and would her mummy be there? She said she didn't want to go if her mummy wasn't there to hold her.

Julie and Penny walked in as the girls were talking. Susie climbed onto Penny's knees. "Mummy, Beth said in heaven we'll be able to pat lions and wolves. They'll be tame, and there'll be beautiful homes for us to live in. She said the grass is very green, and the fruit is enormous, and Jesus will be there to wipe away my tears. But, Mummy, I don't want Jesus to wipe away my tears. I want you to, Mummy," Susie begged.

Penny looked at Julie, pleading with her eyes for help. She held the wasted little form close in her arms.

Julie wondered if what she was about to say would be too hard for such a little girl to understand, and she didn't want to frighten her. She took a deep breath and said a quick, silent prayer before she started.

"She will, sweetheart. When Jesus comes in the clouds with all His angels, Mummy and you will go to heaven together."

"But Mummy said I'm very sick, and I'm going to die and go to heaven. That's right, isn't it, Mummy?' She started to cry. "Please, Mummy, I don't want to go without you."

"Susie, listen to Auntie Julie," said her mother as she stroked the child's golden hair.

Julie tried again. "Susie, when you die, it's like going to sleep, and when Jesus comes, you'll wake up, and Mummy will be there with you. You won't go ahead of Mummy, in any way or form. That will be okay, won't it?"

Susie nodded and smiled through her tears at her mother, who now cried silently within, with a pain so great that she felt her heart would break.

# Chapter 18

# Arrest

Albert watched the news carefully. He wore his customary frown, which puckered his forehead and knitted his thick brows. Janet noticed he wore this expression more and more of late and wondered if he wasn't well. She went to talk to him, but he snapped at her to be quiet.

She looked out the kitchen door and watched the visiting birds feed on grain that he had placed out earlier.

As Albert watched the news, it continually reported the COVID-19 pandemic across the world. He snapped it off and stared out the window.

"Dad, Mum! We're off!" Anita called as she walked past the room. "We're letterboxing the Chatsworth area for the upcoming youth rally."

"How long will you be, dear?" Janet asked as she headed to the front door to say goodbye.

"When we finish, we'll go to Sister Maria's meeting in the city," Tommy answered.

Janet caught her breath, and Anita swung around to see if her father had heard in the kitchen. Tommy wondered what he'd said wrong.

When in the car, Tommy asked, "Didn't you want your father to know about Sister Maria's meeting?"

"Well, Dad's been really cranky. Mum said not to talk to him about it as it wasn't worth the fuss. I get the feeling there's something else going on. Mum and I haven't worked it out, but I dare say we will in time," she explained.

They pulled up on Justin Street with its lovely, shady trees and old, stylish homes with large gardens and lawns.

"We have this block and the next one on the right to do," Tommy said. "I thought when we finish, we could leave the car at your dad's police station and catch the train. The cops at the station wouldn't mind, would they?"

"I wouldn't think so," she answered.

At the first house, a dog sat silently near the letterbox, and when they leaned forward to place their leaflet in, he let out a huge bark and jumped toward them with the intention of biting. Luckily, his bark made Tommy pull his hand back just in time.

"I think we'll throw them on the ground," Anita said, shaking.

"No, the dogs will get them. Let's pray about it," Tommy answered, and he lowered his head and prayed for protection for both of them.

A few houses up, loud voices could be heard as a man and woman screamed at each other. A little farther on, a young girl ran out of a house and jumped on the back of a motorbike. The rider looked really tough. The girl's mother screamed at her to get back, or she would get it when her father came home. The woman saw them, snatched the flyer, and marched back in.

"Well, that's great," Tommy said. "But she has it; that's the main thing, I suppose."

"Yes, and if she comes to the meeting, she might get some help," Anita said. "She certainly needs it by the look of her daughter."

It was Sunday morning, and most of the people were inside because of the virus. Some were attending church through Zoom on their computers or TV. Dogs barked from their backyards or from within the houses.

***Go in here for a bit," he said. "I have orders to go to a building up the road and arrest a terrorist group. You must stay here for at least thirty minutes, and then it should be safe for you to go on.***

In the next block, they met an old lady watering her garden. "Yes, I know I should be inside because of the virus, but the garden needs watering, and I am interested in the leaflet you are letterboxing." They shared with her their news.

Others called out, "Can't you read the sign, mate? No junk mail!"

When Anita and Tommy arrived at the Chatsworth Police Station, Albert was there.

"Dad, I didn't know you were at work today." Anita greeted her father.

"Well, I am, aren't I!" he snapped.

"Mr. Smith, is it all right if we leave the car here?" Tommy asked. "We thought it would be easier to catch a train into the city."

"I'm going that way now. Hold on, and I'll get my keys," Albert mumbled.

They travelled on the Great Western Highway to the inner city. Two streets from the small room where Sister Maria and others were to meet,

Albert stopped his police car in front of a Catholic church and told the kids it was dangerous for them to go farther.

"Go in here for a bit," he said. "I have orders to go to a building up the road and arrest a terrorist group. You must stay here for at least thirty minutes, and then it should be safe for you to go on. Now, Anita, promise you'll stay here for at least thirty minutes," he demanded.

She nodded, and the two stepped out of the car, waving to her father as he drove off. Anita wondered how he knew where in the city to take them. Had he heard what Tommy said earlier that morning? As she thought about it, more police cars drove past, and choppers passed above, all heading in the same direction as her father's car. *Oh, dear! Here we go again*, she thought.

The church had just finished its Sunday service. It was a tall, old, stately cathedral with tall steeples and a bell tower. Inside, the huge stone walls had stained-glass windows depicting Bible stories. The building was long and wide. There was an aisle down the middle and two alongside the walls. In the front behind the font was a stone river, with water that ran and trickled over waterfalls, with many wonderful carvings on its stone banks. It depicted the river of life.

Anita and Tommy walked past the beautiful windows slowly and studied the stories they told. They left through a side door. The half-hour was up, and they decided to walk to their meeting. It would have started by now.

* * *

The meeting with Sister Maria was in progress when Albert's police car silently pulled up. He sat, hesitating, as his throat tightened. An ache behind his eyes throbbed and made it hard for him to focus. He hated what he was about to do, but he had to carry out orders, especially these.

Sister Maria and her friends were breaking a number of restrictions for the virus, but Albert knew this was different. Sister Maria had turned against her beloved papacy and their creeds and laws.

Sister Maria and her friends were on their knees when suddenly, from nowhere, came a terrible crash. Men in uniform charged through the front door and dragged all in the room outside to a police wagon and waiting cars, then sped off.

The black choppers above glided away as quickly as they came. They could be seen individually manoeuvring between the city's buildings on surveillance duty.

Anita and Tommy arrived to find an empty room. Where were their friends?

# Chapter 19

# Baptism

Albert watched the news, as was his habit, but he kept his ears open to all conversation in his household the following Saturday evening. He hoped his family wasn't aware of what had happened to Sister Maria and her nun friends. Over the past week, he hadn't heard any news about the missing nuns.

The newsreader Max Hiller announced that the presidential election in America was in progress. The event was filmed across the world. The president stood in front of the White House and addressed a huge crowd, mostly unmasked.

The president called out, pointing to heaven. "He's the boss, the one in charge. We must let God lead us. He knows best. Let us get back to church."

A roar went up spontaneously like thunder. "Back to church," they roared.

There was still no report on the nuns' arrest, which was a relief to Albert.

* * *

Anita, Tommy, and Brad quietly left the house and headed to the youth rally that they had been advertising with their letterboxing. Anita was glad Brad came—not as a door bouncer, but as a participant this time. The program was to be held at Richmond's cricket oval that was opposite the shops on the main street. For this very special and important event, a large crowd was expected.

When they arrived, the sleepy little suburb was alive with traffic moving in the direction of the oval. They had to park many blocks away and walk. The program wasn't to start for another hour, but most of the appropriately-spaced seats—because of the virus—were already taken. Some people were setting up their own seats under the shop verandas across from the oval.

After walking around, they found seats and, thankfully, sat down. It was a dry, mild evening, and they waited quietly and watched as other youth assembled.

Eventually, a youth leader stood. "Hi, my name is Tony Adams. I'm a leader from the Inner- City Youth Mission. We recently went overseas to help Russia." He showed pictures of many projects and happy volunteers' smiling faces. There were pictures of the villages and people they had helped. Smiling, he announced, "Our youth group will now lead us in songs of praise."

After several uplifting songs, Tony led in prayer. "Today, I wish to talk about the three angels' messages in Revelation chapter 14," he announced. "The first angel summons humanity to worship the Creator God, who made the heavens and the earth and all that's in it. We come to realise worship is the key element in this cosmic conflict. God's people will worship their Creator exclusively. They will follow His Word in the Bible and keep His commandments. They will not follow man and his traditions and dictates.

"The second angel declared Babylon had fallen. In Scripture, Babylon is a political-religious power that rebels against God. This power relies on civil power rather than divine power to achieve its goals. The angel depicts this corrupt political-religious power forcing its dogmas and day of worship onto communities of the world. We are now witnessing this power with the enforcement of Sunday laws in America, and soon Australia. We will also see its literal fall. The angel called, "Come out of her, my people!" he explained to the quiet, listening crowd. "We must come out of this corrupt system! We must come out of all churches because they have become takers of this system!" he called.

"The message of the third angel is a wake-up call to us right now. It vividly describes the experience of those who willingly accept the mark of the beast. They will drink of the wine of God's fury."

He looked around and continued. "Choose this day whom you will serve. Cleanse yourself today by confessing your sins to Jesus and giving your life to Him. The Holy Spirit will not enter an unfit vessel."

He prayed and then made an altar call for all those who desired to serve the Lord.

The preacher quietly spoke to them as they came forward. "No matter if you are mocked or beaten, remember God is there. Remain calm if you are scorned and rejected by your family and friends. You will be rejected for God's sake. Come forward and dedicate your life to Jesus while there's still time," he said quietly into his microphone. "That's right; come up; yes … come and give your life to Jesus."

Soon, it seemed all the people present were standing, some at the front, others where they sat for lack of room. Brad was the first to step forward, followed by Anita and Tommy.

Tommy's family had already made their stand, but Tommy wanted to make an individual dedication of service to God.

Anita had given her life to Jesus at Sister Maria's but also wanted to make a public dedication of her faith. She stood with tears streaming down her face. Holding her big brother's hand, she realised what it meant for Brad and his job.

Their father was against this movement. He and the government classed people like this as dissenters and terrorists against the state. This meeting would be classed as treason. Brad would be in big trouble and would definitely lose his job.

The preacher continued. "Let us now pray. Dear Jesus, today we have seen the outpouring of the Holy Spirit. Be with these young people as they go out and witness for You. Be with them as they listen to Your Holy Spirit in their daily lives. Cleanse and purify them for Your service, Lord Jesus. Oh! Come into our hearts, Lord Jesus. There is room in our hearts for Thee. Amen."

* * *

The following morning, crowds of young people stood on the Hawkesbury riverbank and watched fifty men in white shirts, waist-deep in water. They stood in a long line down the river as the youth waded in and stood quietly beside them.

A song went up amongst those who witnessed the scene. "All to Jesus, I surrender, I surrender all to Thee," they sang.

The preacher spoke for a few minutes, and then the youth were lowered backward into the water. The crowd watched in awe as wave after wave of young people stepped into the water and took their turn in being baptised.

Anita, Tommy, and Brad now stepped forward and stood quietly in the water. Anita whispered and looked to heaven, "Jesus, I surrender. Please make me a fit vessel, I pray."

* * *

Sometime after the election, Anita and Tommy sat quietly listening to the news.

The reporter explained to the viewers. "World leaders met with the pope at the General Assembly for the World Sustainable Development. Hand in hand, church and state have united, and the Constitution of America no longer exists." He practically shouted into the cameras. "The First Amendment in America's Constitution, which dealt with religious freedom and was set up by their forefathers, has been completely removed." He continued to read as footage of the event was shown.

They watched the president of America speak to his people. "The World Council of Churches and the United Nations are requesting all nations to follow. This is totally necessary for world peace."

The Australian prime minister was next. "The people of Australia, through a referendum, have shown the government they agree with the new international laws," he said. "Parliament has voted that Australia will follow the United Nations in the next three months. We will introduce and integrate society under the same laws as passed in America. These laws are for the good of mankind across the world. This is the only way to restore the planet and have peace and harmony for our children's future."

"This is Max Hiller, signing off for Australia Broadcasting Live news."

# Chapter 20

# Child Preacher

Time passed, and it was October and spring in Australia. Eddy and Pat were sitting in their lounge room when their daughter came over. Her parents went to church on Saturday mornings, so she had waited until early evening to arrive. Roslyn brought Jason, their grandson, to visit them. He was going to stay for the evening.

"Now be a good boy, won't you," Roslyn said as she kissed her son goodbye. "Dad, you know what happened? When Jason heard Grandpa was going to the Spring Festival, he had to come and stay." Over her shoulder, she called, "Mum, I'll pick Jason up tomorrow afternoon."

Pat and Eddy stood with their grandson as they waved goodbye to their daughter. It wasn't often Roslyn allowed her children to sleep over; after all, she and her husband, Darren, didn't believe the things they were taught as children, so why build unnecessary bonds between her parents and their boys?

"Come on, Jason, let's go in and have something to eat. It's getting late, and we don't want to miss the parade, do we?" Pat said.

After dinner, Eddy helped young Jason get ready. "Here we go, mate," Eddy said as he helped Jason into his coat and pulled his grandson's woollen cap over his ears.

"Ah! Grandpa, not like that—see, above my ears," young Jason said as he adjusted it.

Eddy laughed and looked up at Pat. "See, Grandma and I are dressed warmly as well."

Hornsby, where Eddy and Pat lived, was an old suburb of Sydney. In October each year, the town held a Spring Festival, and the main street was closed. Floats and clowns travelled down its thoroughfare, and people held stalls on footpaths, while others played musical instruments and danced on the streets, but this year was different.

Police lined the streets and stood in shop doorways, making sure all were abiding by the new social-distancing laws.

Eddy stood Jason on a table near the footpath's edge so he could get a better view of the parade. "Look, Jason, a brass band."

Jason marched on the spot and nodded. "Oh! Look over there in the corner, Grandpa, it's a clown, and there's another one, and another one." Jason laughed at the clowns as they passed. "Look, Grandpa," he squealed in delight and pointed to several floats as they went by. They had children depicting nursery rhymes.

"Look, mate, at those floats with pretty girls, and all the food from crops."

Then a Scottish pipe band marched by, its pipes squawking a tune. Jason placed his hands over his ears in fright and looked up at his grandpa.

"It's okay, mate," Eddy laughed. "They're noisy, aren't they?"

Soon all the floats, bands, and clowns in the parade disappeared around a corner.

A group of local people from all the different Protestant churches assembled together at the top of the street. They were marching in the parade and meant business as this was their way of protesting against those who were refusing to agree with the state green laws and the family rest day. They felt if all citizens joined together, God would bless them and heal the world. They held banners expressing their many views.

Jason stood on the table and watched in fascination. Down the end of the street, a young girl started to play her guitar and sing country and western songs. Jason held Grandpa's shoulder so he could keep his balance while he stood on tiptoes to see what was happening.

Suddenly, Jason began to sing. He sang quietly, then louder and stronger, until the street was filled with the sweet, pure melody from a small boy's voice, a voice that sounded like an angel from above.

***Jason stopped, looked at the crowd, raised his little arms, and started to preach.***

Eddy and Pat stood there amazed. They had never heard their grandson sing anything before. They knew their daughter hadn't sent him to singing classes, so where did he learn this song? It wasn't school, as he was too young to attend.

People started to move closer, to see and hear the child. All stood silent and transfixed in the moment.

Jason stopped, looked at the crowd, raised his little arms, and started to preach.

"Fear God and give glory to him, for the hour of his judgment has come. Worship Him who made heaven and earth, and the sea, and the fountains of waters. If any man worship the beast and his image and receive his mark in their forehead or hand, he shall drink the wrath of God. God's people are commandment-keeping people with the testimony of Jesus. Come out of the false system now and be saved," he called.

Pat knew without a doubt that God was speaking through her grandson. He was quoting from the Bible. Here was a child too young to read and who had never heard Jesus' name spoken in his household, singing and preaching about Jesus' second coming. She looked over at Eddy and caught his eye. He looked back at her with a face white with fear and awe.

The crowd became very quiet, their faces angry. They turned and walked away, mumbling together.

The Protestants from many churches in the district stopped and listened to Jason preach. They became furious and hissed amongst themselves.

One whispered. "Once again, a child, a small child at that, is telling us what to do."

"Well, he may be, but I am not listening. The kids have too much to say today, and what would they know? They spend all their time on their iPads playing demonic games."

"They are delusional," replied another.

"What is wrong with his parents? They need to take his iPad off him," whispered another.

"Yes, for life, and give him hard work around the house like we had to do," grumbled an old man.

A young woman stepped forward. "Well, let's march to the hall. We need to sign the government forms, agreeing with the new laws. If enough of us do this, we will receive God's blessing, and turn the tide of corruption, and turn the virus that is now at plague proportions across the world.'

The organisers of the festival had made arrangements for folk attending to do the same, and many of the crowd now moved down to the hall. The government had told them only those who sign would receive the new future monetary system to buy and sell.

All the while, police kept the crowd at a safe distance from each other. Some refused and were given fines right there on the spot. Others threw punches at the police, and a scuffle followed. The offenders were immediately thrown into police vans that lined the street corners. The crowd stopped for a moment, then walked around the offenders and marched on, intent with what they were about to do.

Quickly, Pat and Eddy left the festival and retreated to their home with their little preacher.

Early the next morning, the phone rang. It was Roslyn, and she was furious.

"Mum, my friend Lynn was at the festival and told me what happened with Jason. How dare you go against our wishes! We told you we weren't interested in all that stuff." She changed her tone and asked moodily, "But how did you do it so quickly? I believe he sang and quoted a portion of the Bible?"

"We didn't, and you're right; we had Jason for about one hour before the festival and certainly didn't have time to teach him anything."

"Well, who did? And how did he learn all of that stuff? Lynn said he sang like an angel, and it was really incredible how he spoke loudly and clearly as if he had great authority, and all from such a little boy."

"I know, dear. Dad and I believe it was a miracle. You know, Jason didn't remember a thing after it happened. Roslyn, you can't run away from God; He loves you and your family. Don't leave it too long before you come back."

Roslyn, much agitated, screamed into the phone, "Mum, we aren't coming back. You never give up! We don't want to see or hear from you both, ever again! Do you hear me, Mum? Leave us alone!" She hung up and collapsed in angry tears. *If Mum only knew, she would understand why God couldn't forgive them for their past*, she thought.

Pat, too, collapsed in tears and prayed. "Jesus, why does Roslyn reject You? Lord, woo her back to You, please, Jesus. Let her understand You love and care for her, and she can come to You with all her worries, cares, and guilt. Jesus, in Your lovely name, we pray. Amen."

Eddy came in and found Pat crying. He sat down and listened to what had happened.

"I think we should go to Adelaide and visit your mother. She is getting old, and we won't have her for much longer. Ring and book a flight for this weekend." He quickly turned and went outside. Over his shoulder, he said as he left, "Don't worry about Roslyn, she'll get over it."

*Eddy always takes everything so casually*, Pat thought with a heavy, saddened heart. How she wished it could be different with Roslyn. She wanted so badly to make it right with her daughter.

Eddy climbed on his ride-on mower and started to mow furiously up and down the lawns. He was heartbroken, but he was determined not to let anyone see his tears. No way; men don't cry.

# Chapter 21

# Drones

Albert sat in his office, the pain behind his eyes indicating a migraine was on the way. How he wished things were different. He would dearly love to be retired and peacefully occupied in his garden. He thought about his situation and his family. Janet would always follow him. Poor, timid Janet, who always did as he said, but things were changing. Brad had made his stand with his sister for Saturday worship, and Janet might follow the children. How he wished he had never allowed Anita to go out with Tommy. He was sure things would have been different if Tommy hadn't been on the scene. He had hoped Brad would take up the Freemason Order and the future New World Program. Brad would now be pursued as a terrorist and possibly be executed. He had to get him away. He must send Brad to Iran. Strange, but it would be safer there, and he knew the person he had to contact to make it possible.

Albert's head throbbed, and his eyes hurt, but he must do what he must do to save his son from himself, and this was the only way. He picked up the phone and dialled.

* * *

Brad entered his room and noticed a letter on his bed. Janet fussed nervously as she placed clean clothes in his dresser drawers. She took a quick sideways look at her son as he read the letter. Her heart sank in fear when she noticed his face.

"What's the matter, dear? Is the news bad?"

Brad didn't answer his mother but handed her the official letter and went outside. She sank on the bed, and as she read, deep, choking sobs racked her body. She couldn't tell Brad, but she knew who was responsible for his sudden transfer.

Brad went out to a large gum tree on the back lawn and sat on his favourite bench chair, sheltering under the tree's large branches. He sat there praying. Janet, her eyes swollen, joined her son. She realised that he was praying, so she waited quietly next to him. She sat deep in her own thoughts until Brad looked up.

"I came out here because you can never tell if your home is bugged." He realised he sounded corny. He changed the subject. "When's Dad due home?"

"He's away until Monday evening. He's at that three-monthly convention thing at Springwood Convent," she said with much venom, which surprised Brad.

"And Anita and Tommy?" he asked.

"They've gone to Sutcliffe Christian Youth Camp for the school break-up. They left this morning and will be there for eight days. They won't be back before you leave." She caught her breath. "It's so sudden, Brad. How can they expect you to leave so soon, and by Monday morning?"

"It must be a huge emergency. I'll spend the evening with the kids at Sutcliffe and say my goodbyes there. Don't worry, I'll be back tomorrow night, and you and I will go out for dinner."

He hugged his mum, who cried softly into his shoulder. She looked up with tears on her cheeks and once again spoke with hostility and venom. "Your father won't be back in time to say his goodbyes."

"Does he know where the kids have gone?" Brad asked.

Janet shook her head. "No, we kept it a secret. He thinks they're down the beach with Tommy's family."

Brad nodded and kissed his mother's head.

On his way to the Sutcliffe Christian Youth Camp, Brad stopped at the Richmond Air Force Base to pick up things from his desk. He pulled up at the gates and placed his card into the slot. The boom gate lifted, and he drove across the parking lot to a large, two-story timber building. He parked and quickly walked to his office, placed another card into the door lock, and entered.

The empty office was lined with desks holding computers. *I wonder what job my squadron is on*, he thought. Just then, many drones like a swarm of locusts rose in the air. He rushed to a window facing the parade ground and noticed it was the "Chemical Weapon Drone Squadron."

Running up the stairs two at a time to the control room, he pulled on his jumper and straightened himself. Entering the room and taking a deep breath, he tried to look casual.

"Hi! Jim, I see the Chemical Weapon Drones are leaving for a raid. Do you know where they're sending them?" he asked casually as he watched from the window.

The young man who had been giving instructions to the drones' operator looked up. "I thought you were on leave."

"Yes, I am. I'm picking up a few things," Brad answered—and he thought. *It seems as if they don't know about my transfer.*

"Is it an important mission?" he asked. He knew it was illegal to give out information to those not involved in the operation.

"Terrorists," answered the other officer, forgetting Brad wasn't part of the operation that morning. "I believe it's a dangerous group. They're up at Sutcliffe's campgrounds. The squadron has been given orders to use the Yellow Belly Drones. It'll be interesting to see how efficient it's going to be in such cases."

"Is that so," Brad said as casually as he could, now edging to the door, his heart racing. He knew Yellow Belly was a specially-designed gas that killed all in its path but left buildings intact. He rushed to the parking lot and hit his mobile phone. He hoped his sister would answer. "Oh, God, please help me to be in time," he prayed.

The swarm of drones could be seen heading to their destination, which was only a few kilometres away.

"Hi, Brad," Anita answered. "Tommy and I have been watching your squadron's new drones heading this way. What are they doing, big brother? Heading off to some dangerous destination, I bet," she laughed.

"No, no. You must listen. You're in great danger. Get everyone out of the campgrounds now, and run to the creek. Do you hear me? Go now. They're about to kill you all. Do you hear? Get away now!" he yelled into his mobile phone.

"Brad, we're on the edge of a creek about half a kilometre down the mountain. We're with four of our friends. The others are in the main hall, having worship. Some may still be in their dormitories."

"We're too far away. Brad, the drones are now overhead!" yelled Anita. "What should we do?"

As she spoke, Tommy phoned his mate, Josh. The four with them also rang friends at the main campground. Yells and calls went up as the news was conveyed to everyone.

All ran out of the buildings. The drones were above. It was too late. Specially-designed gas that seemed to come from the drones' undercarriage spread over the people below, who stood fixed in fear. The gas spread over the buildings and the surrounding areas, over their teachers with their families with small children and babies. All were crying and choking on the fumes. Soon, hacking coughs and projectile vomiting followed, as the people on the ground curled in agonising pain and died.

The drones were now completely out of sight. The mission completed, the drones were digitally guided back to base. The operators were not fully aware of the devastation they had caused and the terrible, agonising deaths those below suffered.

All Anita and Tommy and their friends could see from below was yellow gas covering and engulfing the campgrounds and buildings. The drones moved quietly and swiftly. They could hear clearly the agonised cries of their friends.

Brad, driving frantically toward his sister, also witnessed the yellow gas. "Place something over your faces in case the fumes reach you and head for the road! I'm not far from you now!" he yelled.

The young people clamped their hats over their noses and mouths and pushed through the lantana and undergrowth as they half ran, half stumbled to the road. They scrambled through a tall growth of lantana near the road edge, only to be met by police with drawn guns.

With her heart racing, Anita yelled into her phone, "We're trapped, Brad! We're trapped! The cops have us!"

There were many police, their cars blocking the road access. "Well, look what we have here. In the van, you lot. Move it! Do you hear what I say? Just get a move on!" one of the officers roared.

Brad was stopped at another roadblock farther down the mountain. Here, three police cars were strung across the road. Police stood outside their cars with hands on their guns still in holsters.

"Sorry, but you can't pass. Go back the way you came," an officer bullied. Brad flashed his ID card. "Sorry, Captain Smith, but this is a terrorist alert, and you know what that means."

"Yes, yes, that's okay, mate, but can you tell me if any of these menaces have been captured alive," Brad asked, trying to act indifferent.

"Yes, there were six of them, just up the road. They won't get away again, sir, you can be sure of that. They're being taken this very moment as we speak to the Springwood Convent. It's been converted into a detention centre, you know," the officer said in a talkative manner.

"Yes, I'm well aware," Brad snapped. He turned his car quickly and sped off. He knew another way to St Mary's.

* * *

He sped into the convent yard, swung the car around the drive, and screeched to a stop in front of a van holding the kids.

"You can hand the kids over," he said as he flashed his ID.

A man in the shadows spoke as several police officers moved forward. "I'm very sorry, Captain, but you, too, are under arrest for terrorist actions."

# Chapter 22

# Grand Master

At midnight, forty men dressed as Ku Klux Klan members arrived at St Mary's Convent. These government officials and public servants came in secret. They entered the foyer in their Ku Klux Klan robes and headgear and received their candles in their holders. They knew not who was next to them, and they didn't want to know.

They entered the courtyard with its wooden cross in the centre. Flapping from balconies and high stands were banners displaying the half moon and sun sign. All placed their candles with their holders onto the stands.

The men stood quietly and waited for the Grand Master to enter the balcony above. When he did, he held his hand high, displaying the secret Jesuit salute. They followed, repeating after him the secret Jesuit creed.

After the Grand Master made his speech on world conditions and how all present played a key part in these matters, he clapped his hands, and the party started. Scantily-dressed girls carried trays of food and alcoholic drinks. The Grand Master settled back and drank much more than usual. Tonight, he was about to stage a show different from all in the past. The more he drank, the more his new idea seemed logical. He would bring in the youth who were arrested as terrorists earlier that evening and let them watch—it would teach them all a good lesson.

The prisoners were brought down from their rooms to the entrance foyer. Double doors were opened so they could look into the courtyard. They stood in the shadows of the arched veranda and watched. The scene taking place gave them such a shock. All were silent, too fearful to speak. Brad placed his arms around his sister, who was shaking so hard her legs could hardly hold her.

The scene wasn't a shock at all to Brad, and Tommy had heard in his church of such gatherings. The men's drunken laughter became coarse, and Brad feared for his sister's safety. All six stood in abject fear. They were in great danger.

Time went on—for how long they didn't know—then guards pushed a person past them, dragging their prisoner to the cross and tying her hands to the crossbar. It was Sister Maria; poor, thin, elderly Sister Maria. They tore the back of her shirt, and someone came into the courtyard with a whip.

The Ku Klux Klan men raised their hands and gave the secret salute. They yelled over and over, "The Grand Master! The Grand Master!" All realised the Grand Master was about to execute justice on the poor nun, now strung on the cross with her back bare.

The whip came down, and a cry went up, a cry that was in unison with the one afflicted. Anita realised it was she who had cried. She shoved a fist into her mouth and watched as the whip came down again. Sister Maria jerked, and her lower body arched backward. Soon blood gushed from deep cuts which exposed her ribs. Her frail body slumped, and excruciating pain gave way to darkness. Orders were given to untie her and take her back to the cellar.

The Grand Master stood by as if he wasn't sure what to do. He watched closely as they moved her.

Sister Maria opened her eyes and whispered weakly. Only the Grand Master caught what she said: "Albert, I forgive you because you don't know what you're doing."

He reeled backward. How did she know? Who else knew his secret? Only Father Frank knew who he was, or so he thought. Grinding his fingers into his temples as a piercing pain took over and his eyes burnt, Albert slumped forward and followed those carrying the nun.

Anita caught her breath as she watched him walk toward them. The Grand Master—it was her father, her beloved father, whom all her life she had idolised. She loved him dearly. As a small child, she could always tell his footsteps down the passage. She knew all his little mannerisms, and she knew a migraine was bothering him.

As they pushed passed, she cried in a whisper, "Oh, Daddy, Daddy, what have you done? Please, Daddy, help me. Don't leave me, Daddy. Please don't leave us like this." She collapsed in Brad's arms, sobbing deeply.

Brad had known about his father for some time. He followed Albert's progress past them with an impassive face.

Albert went back to the room that Father Frank kept for him and sank on his bed as the migraine took over. Why were the children here? They must have been at the campgrounds. And who else heard his daughter's cries, he wondered.

* * *

Albert woke in the early hours of the morning and went straight to Sister Maria's cell. He realised what he had done. It was still dark and especially dark in the cellar. He chose not to turn lights on, partly because of his throbbing head and partly because he didn't want anybody to see him. He negotiated the stairs without a light and entered the main door to the large underground cellar that was divided into prison cells.

He stood, trying to fathom what he saw. The cellar was in darkness, but Sister Maria's cell was bathed in light. Albert knew there was only one central light switch that turned on all four lights across the whole room. *Perhaps the man in her cell was holding a torch*, Albert thought to himself; *How did he get in there? Is he one of the guards checking on her? It can't be as I have the only keys in my pocket*. He moved silently forward.

The man was talking quietly to Sister Maria. There wasn't any torch; the room was softly lit with a light of its own. The man leaned forward and examined her deep cuts. Gently placing his hands on her, the cuts were healed. Then the stranger disappeared. Albert stood in complete darkness.

He stumbled back to the main door and fumbled for the light switch. All four dingy, grubby lights came on in unison. Albert moved fearfully toward Sister Maria. Was he going mad and dreaming all of this? *Of course, that's what's happening,* he decided.

Unlocking her cell, Albert entered. Sister Maria was asleep. He pulled back her blankets, and as she lay on her stomach, he could see her exposed back. Her torn shirt, still bloodied, hung below the top of her skirt. Now, her back was clean. There wasn't any blood or welts or cuts to be seen. Had he been mistaken the night before, and none of this happened.

*If it didn't happen, then my son and daughter weren't there either. That was just as well,* he thought. Drunk and confused, he decided to go back to bed and sort it out in the morning.

Unseen by Albert, in the adjoining cells were the other nuns who were arrested with Sister Maria. They lay quietly on their beds, praying for Sister Maria, and were watching and witnessing all. They saw the angel heal Sister Maria, and Albert check on her. Albert, the Grand Master, his face exposed to all, who had imprisoned his own children.

* * *

The next morning, Albert realised he was in great danger. He had exposed his position to many. He knew what he had to do. His Islamic heritage, even though a few generations removed, gave him the mindset necessary for the actions needed, but first, he must take care of his family. Anita's pleading voice kept coming back to him, making it impossible for him to think. He must get to his office and make arrangements while he could.

He drove down the Great Western Highway to Sydney and found himself at Bondi Beach. The beach had always calmed him. He sat with his car window open and smelt the sea. Volunteers were at work, packing sandbags along the shoreline, making the temporary sea break a meter high. Global warming was melting snow at the North Pole, with the sea rising and squally weather predicted. Construction work was taking place farther down the beach for a more permanent breakwater.

The turbulent roar of the waves became louder. Albert watched as the breakers rolled in, crashed, and flattened out. Nearby, a radio squawked, telling the same news it always told. He heard the announcer talk about a mass killing of terrorists at the Sutcliffe campgrounds. He quickly backed his car and drove to his destination.

When he arrived at the police station, he locked himself in his office. He picked up the phone and made arrangements for Brad. He would be flown out to Iran that very evening. He made more calls, making arrangements for Anita, Tommy, and their friends. They would be driven to a youth detention centre in the outback of Australia at Wilcannia, an isolated town made up mainly of Aborigines. They would be safe there and would be made to stay until they changed their ideas. He then wrote a letter explaining all to his wife, Janet. He placed the letter in an envelope and drove home.

When he arrived home, he pushed the garage remote control. The door rolled up slowly. Janet's car was there, which meant she was home. He entered his home by the door through the garage and sidled into the billiard room. He slipped into the small kitchen-cum-bar room and reached up to a high cupboard, bringing down a box. He placed it on the pool table with his letter. The letter would explain to Janet what she needed to do.

He could hear Janet calling him as she went from room to room. "Albert, I have terrible news for you. It's about the Sutcliffe Christian Youth Camp. Albert, where are you, dear?" she called as she went from the lounge room to the bedroom, then down the passage that led to the billiard room. Albert could tell she was frantic.

She walked into the billiard room. "Albert, the children; we must find …"

Albert stood with an expression of agony on his face, pressing his temple not with his fingers but with a revolver.

"Albert!" she screamed. "What are you doing? I need you, dear. Please, dear, I need you. The children need you."

It was clear at that moment what he needed to do. Two shots rang out. One for Janet, and then another for himself, straight through his temple. They lay in pools of blood, dead.

There was silence for a moment or two, then the kookaburras cackled, and the parrots squawked as they waited for breakfast. Mist hung in the mountains, and all was at peace, except for man's plight.

## Chapter 23

# The Fire Kept Burning

The girls were held prisoners on the second floor at St Mary's. Their meals were eaten in the small dining room on this floor. The boys were captive on the third floor. Anita and one of her friends from the Sutcliffe Camp shared a room. Anita sat on the edge of her bed, looking out the window. It looked across the front garden, the roundabout, and the entrance gates. She was glad it did, as she thought it would be terrible if she had one of the rooms looking across the court garden and the terrible cross that stood at its centre. *Poor Sister Maria,* she thought. Anita couldn't believe what had happened the night before to the elderly nun.

***Two men walked toward the car. One was being led, with handcuffs on. He turned and looked up toward her window. It was Brad.***

Voices below caught her attention. She leaned close to the window to see who was out there. A black Mercedes drove through the gates and parked. Two men walked toward the car. One was being led, with handcuffs on. He turned and looked up toward her window. It was Brad, and the other man, when he saw what he was doing, roughly pushed him into the car. The car quickly drove out the gates.

Anita flopped down on her bed and started to cry again, rubbing her already swollen eyes. "It was Brad out there, Jane. They've taken him away, and he was handcuffed," she wailed.

Jane jumped up to see, but he was gone. "Who took him away?" she asked with eyes boggling.

"They pushed him in a big black car and drove off," Anita choked.

Jane sat next to Anita and held her hand. "I wonder what's going on," she whispered, and then dropped into silence.

Late that evening, there was a knock on their bedroom door. Both girls had been staring silently into the room's darkness while they lay on their beds. They jumped up. Anita snapped on the light and opened the door. Father Frank and another priest stood there.

"Can we come in for a minute? We have something to tell you," Father Frank said with a sneer.

The girls backed away and huddled together, afraid, wondering what was about to happen.

"Anita," he said coldly.

Fear struck Anita's heart, and like a captured bird of prey, she made a desperate attempt to show bravery. She stamped her feet and yelled, "I want to see my father, now! Do you hear me? Get my father this minute! You'll be in real trouble when he hears about this."

"Your father can't come and will never hear about anything," Father Frank sneered.

*Oh no! We are in for it*, Anita thought. She huddled against Jane, hugging her friend tightly. Looking over Jane's shoulder, she gathered more strength. "Where have you taken my brother?"

"Your father has sent Brad overseas. You won't ever see him again."

Anita felt she had been slapped across the face, and she stood numbly, trying to digest what she had been told.

"Now, the news I came to tell you," Father Frank continued in a matter-of-fact fashion, without feeling or expression. "Is this, both your parents are dead. Your father shot your mother and then himself at 10:00 a.m. this morning. There will be an enquiry into the matter."

A hollow scream echoed through the room, and echoed in the corridor and rooms beyond. Anita collapsed onto her bed. "No-o-o-o! No-o-o-o-o!" she screamed.

Father Frank watched without expression, staring at the girl, then spun on his heels and stepped out of the room. The other priest, red-faced and uncomfortable, shut the door quietly behind them.

Anita curled in a fetal position, silent, as shock had set in. Jane lay behind her, holding her tight, and sobbed for her stricken friend.

Late that night, Jane walked silently to the front foyer, which was near the landing on their floor, and spoke to a priest who, with another, was guarding the floor. She spoke quietly to him. The two priests whispered together. They turned to her and nodded. One left and soon arrived with Tommy.

Jane spoke quietly to Tommy and then returned to her room. She shook her friend. "Anita, Tommy is waiting for you."

Anita stood slowly in a wobbly fashion. She leaned on her friend, who guided her to the foyer. Anita staggered to Tommy, collapsing into his arms, and for the first time since she heard the news, sobbed deeply. Tommy held her all evening. He offered comfort and prayers for and with her until a bus arrived the next morning. He and the others in his small group were pushed on board.

As Tommy expected, the ten other youth already in the bus were Islamic. They were all going to a dissenters' camp. *Troublemakers of the State, that's how we've been tagged*, Tommy thought.

The bus travelled over the Blue Mountains and headed west on the highway. Anita sat sadly looking blindly out the window, unaware of her red, swollen eyes or the unchecked tears running down her cheeks. She felt quite numb. It was like she was sleep-walking in a bad dream. She thought of her lovely, kind mother. She couldn't comprehend what she had been told about their deaths. Her parents loved each other. It wasn't real, she thought. Then she remembered what her father had done to Sister Maria and the people at the Sutcliffe Camp. How could her father who had always supported her turn into this unknown, unfeeling, gowned and hooded man? They called him the Grand Master. What did they mean by this? He was always against new churches and groups. How did he get so involved with such strange company? And where were they taking her big brother? These questions occupied her mind, and she didn't notice any of the scenery on the miserable journey.

Tommy watched carefully, noting everything in the bus and also outside. He wanted to know every town and road they travelled, as well as the distance. He watched the others closely. They, too, sat quiet and watchful.

The bus passed through parched countryside. Tall gums flanking the edge of the road gave some shade to a few straggly goats. As Tommy looked across the barren paddocks, he was aware of smoke, and when the bus turned a bend in the road there it was—fire. Flames leaping ten and twenty metres high blazed through the tops of high gum trees that lined the right side of the road ahead of them. Everyone leaned forward to see. A gabble of high-pitched voices broke out as they spoke back and forth to each other.

"Look," yelled a girl, "the fire's jumping to branches in trees across the road."

A boy of about fourteen yelled, "The fire's running and igniting, like fuel has been thrown over it! Wow! I learned about this in school! Eucalyptus oil in gum leaves have this effect when under great heat."

The driver stopped the bus and dialled for help on his mobile. The passengers stepped out of the bus and looked in horror at the fire now racing at rapid speed toward them. Their frightened chatter penetrated the smoke-permeated air.

Tommy looked down the road behind them. The bend in the road was to the left of the bus. At this point the fire jumped the road and roared up the other side in their direction. Next to the bus, on each side of the road was an open, grassy patch that hadn't yet caught fire. The trees behind these patches burst into flames and the bus was surrounded by fire. It roared and thundered through the trees, and the heat was terrible. A blanket of smoke above the trees rose in the sky like a large impregnable wall.

Soon, they heard fire engines heading their way. The youth covered their faces. They coughed and sneezed.

"Into the bus!" the driver called. He encouraged, pulled, probed, and roughly pushed his blinded, spluttering passengers. "Come on, now. Let's hurry. All back to the bus."

All went except Tommy, who paced back and forth. "Lord, You saved us at the camp and at the convent. Surely You haven't brought us out here to die. Please, Lord, save us," he prayed.

The road was blocked, so the fire engines had to drive across paddocks. They could only approach the fire from the other side of the trees.

"Bill, get your boys to hose the bottom of the trees and then slowly up their trunks!" shouted the fire captain over the roar of the flames. "Fred, take your truck to the end of the paddock and hose inwards, and Max, take yours to the other end," he barked.

When all three trucks were in front of the flames, they squirted water from pressurised hoses from the bottom to the top of the flames. The smoke and heat intensified. The fire kept burning. The men kept yelling and hosing. Now the grass close to the bus started to burn.

"Fred, I don't know what we can do! We're making the flames go in the direction of the bus!" screamed the captain.

Tommy kept praying. It was extremely hot, and his eyes were streaming from the smoke. He found it hard to breathe and kept coughing. He was inspired to hold up his arms to heaven and call. "In the name of Jesus, I rebuke you, Satan! Leave now and turn back these flames!" He ran to the front of the bus and called, "In the name of Jesus, you are rebuked and defeated, Satan, so turn these flames back the way they came!"

He kept calling in this manner until he had rebuked Satan in the name of Jesus on all sides of the bus. He climbed into the bus exhausted, but positive that God and His angels would send Satan packing. Anita patted his arm as he sat down and wiped his streaming eyes.

After a few moments, the flames turned back across the trees, and the firemen moved their engines, as they were in the thick of it and in danger of having their engines destroyed by the huge flames. After about twenty minutes, they were able to make their way up the road to the bus.

The chief fireman, sweaty and very sooty, walked up to the bus driver, grinning. He had an incredible story to share.

"You know," he said, "in all my twenty years of firefighting, I haven't seen anything like it. The fire turned back on itself. Things like this just don't happen, you know," he explained.

"About what time did it turn back?" Tommy asked.

"Twenty minutes ago," the fireman answered.

*That's when I rebuked Satan*, Tommy thought. He spoke in a small voice. "I prayed that the fire would turn back."

"Yes, he did," the driver said. "I saw him walking around the bus with his arms held high, rebuking Satan out loud, in the name of the Lord." The driver laughed in disbelief.

"Well, son, your prayers were answered because it *was* a miracle. I can tell you, if it hadn't happened, we wouldn't have saved you. All our efforts were causing the fire to burn toward the road and you lot. Yes, it certainly was a miracle," continued the chief fire fighter, but he spoke more to himself than the others, as he walked back to his crew.

It had been a hot, long day, and all were exhausted. At seven in the evening it was still light. The bus drove through the town of Wilcannia. It was a sad little town, mostly closed, with heavy bars on all shop windows. Aborigines sat in groups on the edge of the footpath, and watched as the bus passed through their town.

They travelled about another twenty kilometres and came to a creek crossing. It would have been a substantial river, but because of drought the Darling was now a small, barely-running creek. On its wide sandy banks were large willows.

They continued on past vast vegetable gardens. On the road edge and near the gardens were youth returning from their day's work.

Anita, horrified at the sight, leaned closer to Tommy and whispered in his ear. "Look at those boys," she whispered, staring in disbelief at the prisoners.

"Don't stare, Anita. Those soldiers have guns, and they're watching us closely."

All in the bus watched the prisoners, forming a chain gang. Each was chained to the next by the ankle. They stumbled along in a clanging fashion, with despairing expressions.

The bus soon arrived at their destination. The guard at the gate barked. "Where's your identification?" Their driver handed over his papers, and they drove through high gates that immediately slammed shut behind them. A high fence with three rows of razor wire running along the top surrounded the compound. Inside were many timber buildings like army barracks. All in the bus stared at their surroundings, and deep, deep, despair came over them.

## Chapter 24

# Guerrilla Assaults—Lebanon

At Lebanon's border, guerrilla assaults on United States soldiers were taking place. They had caught a captain from one of the ground forces patrols. She was held as a hostage. Her unit knew she would be interrogated. They had to get to her quickly before she was tortured and killed in the rebel's mountain camp.

The ground force crept forward in the bushy undergrowth toward the front of the building. The leading lieutenant signalled to his men to lie still. A soldier was sent behind the building. He threw a hand grenade as hard as he could to the right of the building. The rebel soldiers came out firing automatic machine guns. Bullets flew as they fired and ran in the opposite direction of the explosion.

The ground force lieutenant and two of his soldiers rushed toward the front of the building. They entered and saw rebels. Another round of bullets was fired, killing all the rebels.

"We have the captain," the lieutenant said into his field telephone. "Don't use hand grenades, as we will set up explosives before we leave. I'll explain when back at line. Over and out."

Quickly, they set up many explosives throughout the building and then ran out the front door just as the rebel soldiers outside turned and ran back, firing. When they entered the building, they saw it was too late as the prisoner had escaped, and the guards were dead.

The returning rebels set up their machine guns at a window and shot in the direction of the escaping soldiers. The soldiers dropped to the ground in the undergrowth. The lieutenant pressed the explosive's automatic detonator, leaving them twenty seconds to get out of the area.

"Go, go, go!" the captain yelled. "Move, just move, you lot!"

The soldiers ran as fast as they could, deep into the scrub. A huge explosion with hot, red flames flung debris high into the sky. The soldiers kept running. When back at the road, they regrouped and waited for orders.

"Sir," said the captain on her field telephone, "the terrorists were about to use anthrax virus. If they start this rot, many will be destroyed!"

* * *

Albert's request to transfer his son to the Middle East came to fruition. Brad became a co-pilot for the United Nations Black Hawk helicopter patrol, part of the defence force against guerrilla insurgency.

Another outbreak was taking place. His lead chopper signalled to its partner, "Delta Harry calling Delta Sam, do you hear me? Over."

"Delta Sam, receiving you, over."

"Hit ground force on your left with laser control. Do you copy? Over."

"Roger, over and out."

The second chopper swung hard to the left and swooped on guerrilla soldiers hiding in rocky ravines. Brad's chopper, Delta Harry, did the same as it swung hard to the right. The guerrillas were surprised by the movement; they had never seen these helicopters used in attacks before. They stood for a moment staring—a moment too long. The choppers aimed laser beams at their faces. The beams exploded in their eyes, and agonising screams followed. They writhed on the ground in excruciating pain, as their eyeballs fried in their sockets. The choppers turned and high-tailed it out of there.

War with the United Nations Defence Force had taken on a new dimension. Brad was absolutely horrified. He doubled over and vomited.

Back at his quarters, Brad lay on his bunk, staring at the ceiling. He couldn't forget what had happened that day. A radio was playing next to him, and an American newsreader discussed regional events. Brad listened.

"Lebanon is hell on earth. Many different rebel factions are striking civilians and US Army personnel with American-made weapons. The people of Lebanon think the US is the biggest criminal in the world. It is common to hear chants on the street declaring death to Americans and Zionists. They chant, 'Jews are a cancerous tumour that should be executed.' They also chant, 'We will take over the world.'"

"It certainly is becoming a true religious war," declared the reporter.

*Thanks a lot, Dad, for sending me to this hell-hole*, Brad thought. He then remembered his other Father, and closed his eyes, and prayed. "Please, Lord, this is terrible. I wish to honour You, and I certainly don't want to be part of this war. Please, Lord, get me released from service, somehow, and I thank You for this, in Jesus' name. Amen."

The next morning, he was called to the head office. Standing to attention, he was told about his transfer that was to take place the next day. It was a position with the United Nations Peace Corps in Jerusalem.

*Thank You, Lord. You have remembered me, and so quickly*, he thought.

"Captain, you heard the good news. Now I have to inform you of unpleasant news. We have been notified that your father and mother are dead. Apparently, your father was mentally disturbed. He shot your mother, then himself. Sorry, Captain. That will be all," the Colonel said, not unkindly.

Brad stumbled back to his barracks in shock. He knew that at the end, his father had acted out of character. His mother always told him it was dangerous to belong to secret societies. He now realised his mother knew about his father. *Perhaps this was why she always seemed so nervous*, he thought.

A deep sadness swept over him. He loved both his parents, especially his kind, thoughtful mum. He worried about his sister, Anita. What was his father thinking when he arrested the kids? He felt numb, unable to think, feel, or cry. Fitful sleep eventually took over. Between being awake, then asleep, and then having nightmares, he thought of his sister. She became part of his nightmares. Shock set in and Brad slept through the next day. The coming and going of men in his unit became part of his fitful sleep. He was glad to wake the following morning in the early hours and walk in the desert's cool morning breeze. He was thankful he could cry out through his deep pain to Jesus his Saviour.

When Brad returned to the barracks, he heard Christmas music. He looked at his calendar and realised it was only three weeks away. This made him feel even more lost and lonely.

His friend Steven, an American soldier, noticed how upset he was. "I'm going shopping; want to come?" he asked.

"Okay. Shopping in Beirut will be different!" responded Brad.

"That's for sure," Steven laughed.

* * *

Beirut, the capital of Lebanon, was very old, with many mosques. The city's outskirts had many crumbling buildings, with metal and twisted rods protruding through the rubble, evidence of continued unrest and war in the region. Uniformed American and Australian soldiers walked amongst the people in the city streets and local markets. Brad and Steven sat at a small restaurant on the sidewalk and watched the women chattering together as they passed by, as Western women do at home, but these were Muslims, dressed in black with only their eyes evident.

"Well, mate, it sounds as if you and I might be in trouble. We both work for the United Nations Peace Corps, you in America, and I in Australia, and now we are transferred to the same new posting. Also, both our dads took part in secret societies, and both are now dead," Brad said.

"Yes, and we were both transferred here by who knows who, and now we're being transferred to Jerusalem tomorrow," Steven continued as he took up the story.

"Yes, let's hope the authorities employing us don't know we're secret dissenters against the United Nations' One World Church," Brad replied, frowning. "I have it on good authority we'll be employed as bodyguards and be agents in the CIA. We will be involved in a secret mission for the United Nations. Believe me; they'll be watching us closely. I hope and pray they don't find out about our beliefs."

Steven looked horrified. He glanced away and tried to digest what he had been told. Then, as if it was too much, he changed the subject. As they walked, they talked, soon coming to a church—or maybe it was a temple or mosque; they weren't sure.

Steven raised his arms and began to preach, right in front of the building. "Jesus came and died for a sin-sick world!" People started to gather, speaking amongst themselves. They were angry and threw their arms in the air, shaking their fists at Brad and Steven.

"Mate, you'd better stop. You're not in America, the land of the free," said Brad as he pulled at Steven's arm. "Come on, mate. The crowd's getting really angry. Let's get out of here."

The people picked up stones and threw them at Brad and Steven. The boys ducked and ran. When they were a good distance from the crowd, Brad, out of breath and doubled over, felt angry with Steven. *How dare him to be so foolish,* he thought. He spoke between gulps. "Mate, I think we had better get something straight. From now on, silence is our motto."

# Chapter 25

# Sydney's Night Club

Jacky hadn't forgotten his talk with Sister Maria. Yes, he was one of the people of the night, but he was determined to share Jesus with his people.

He rushed down a dirty narrow lane in Kings Cross. He had received a phone call while at Sister Maria's city mission. A young girl spoke and said it was an emergency. Jacky realised people were scared to contact the police or paramedics.

Jacky entered by the building's back door. It was dark, and he stood trying to focus, realising he had entered a night club, but still wasn't sure about its degree of sleaziness, as it was hard to see. He squinted, and made out at the end of the room a bar, and next to the bar, a pile of mattresses.

A radio in the next room shrieked out the day's news. "New South Wales and Victoria are ablaze. Over two thousand square kilometres of farmland is burning. Over five hundred homes have been wiped out. Fire fighters have come from every state of Australia to help in this emergency. United Nations international fire fighters will arrive this evening with another one hundred planes to hose the hungry, consuming flames," announced the reader.

Jacky's eyes, now adjusted to the darkness, enabled him at last to see. In the middle of the room stood a felt-covered dancing platform with four poles and tables and chairs arranged around all four sides. This must be a pole-dancing club, where scantily dressed girls would dance around the poles in an alluring fashion. These places were the worst of their type, with under-age prostitution rackets usually hidden in their filthy back rooms.

"Please, help me," a female voice murmured. A young girl lay on a much-stained mattress. Her hair clung damply to her sweaty brow. She was obviously very ill. Was it sexual abuse, or was it Corona virus? Jacky knew the flu was at epidemic proportions in the inner-city areas. Should he touch her—and would he get the virus if he did, he wondered? Dropping his head, he prayed. Sister Maria had taught him to take all things to God in prayer. *I wonder where Sister Maria is,* he thought and included a bit about her protection in his prayer as well. Suddenly, he knew what he had to do.

Sister Maria had taught him simple hydrotherapy. Jacky strode to one of the tables and pulled off its cheap, tatty tablecloth. Taking it to the bar sink, he ran cold water over it, then wrung it out loosely and carefully rolled the cloth around the girl's body. She needed to be encased in its cool dampness. Also, a cool cloth was placed around her head. When he was finished, he looked in the other dingy back room but couldn't find anybody. Coming back to the girl, he changed the cloths almost immediately. With her fever they would become a hot steam bath, and he couldn't let this happen. Pulling off another tablecloth, he proceeded to wet, wring, and wrap it around the girl. After a few minutes, the procedure was repeated and kept up until her fever subsided. Jacky kept praying while waiting for a response from his patient.

Leaning back against the wall, Jacky, exhausted, fell asleep. How long he slept, he didn't know. When he awoke, she was lying with open, watchful eyes.

"Did ya ring me?" he asked.

"Yes! Have you checked upstairs?" she whispered.

"No," he said, surprised.

"Go through that door and go upstairs."

Jacky ran up the stairs two at a time and found girls, but to his shock, they were dead. Heart pounding, he ran back to the lower room and rang 000 on the phone at the bar.

"There's three of 'em upstairs. Dead, they are. There's one down 'ere. No, I ain't seen anybody else," he said into the phone.

Replacing the receiver, he turned to the girl. "Have ya seen anybody else?"

"I think there was a cop raid in the early hours. I heard choppers, then cops. There were lots of loud voices, and then it went quiet."

Soon choppers could be heard above, and then ambulance and police sirens racing toward the address. Jacky quietly left the same way he came. He wasn't sticking around to talk to cops. *You can't trust them*, he thought to himself as he ducked between buildings and disappeared, as the people of the night had a habit of doing.

In his hurry, he bumped into a shopping trolley and sent it spinning across the alley. Old Mavis, who was scratching through the wheelie bin, looked up. She grinned a big toothless grin and cackled.

"Sorry, old girl, I'll see ya at the mission. I'm takin' the service," Jacky explained. She grinned even wider and cackled loudly as she nodded her approval.

Jacky rushed down a vacant city street. Since the virus plus recession, a steady stream of city dwellers and shopkeepers had been evacuating the city, leaving many shops closed with heavy metal roller-doors covering their windows. Those still open for business had bars on their windows, and outside stood armed security guards. Further up an alleyway, hidden from the police, a group of young people clustered, buying and selling drugs. In the distance the usual buzz of helicopters could be heard hovering over the city buildings.

Suddenly, a deafening roar heralded a chopper above. The group disappeared as if they were never present. The chopper hovered like a large hawk, ready to pounce on its prey. Jacky watched it manoeuvre between high-rise buildings and then spring into action, chasing a car that sped past as it tried to negotiate side lanes with lots of clutter.

That evening this simple youth, his face lit up and transformed into peace and joy, looked at his people. They were the poorest, most depraved of all humanity, but Jesus loved them and died for them, and Jacky was about to share this good news.

"Have ya felt a little breeze pass over ya face?"

They all grinned and agreed and called. "Yeah! Yeah!"

"Well, the Holy Spirit is the same. First, He comes as a little breeze. He tells ya how to think and speak. Then stronger and stronger, He'll talk with ya, and now you're changed into a beautiful being. Do ya want this to happen?" he asked.

Now they roared their approval. They stamped their feet and laughed as they pointed to each other.

"Let's pray, and I'll tell ya about Jesus," he said. This simple, uneducated youth stood in front of his people. God's Spirit came upon him, and he spoke simply but without his uneducated impediments.

"Our people, the people of the night—well, we've fended for ourselves. We've fought and struggled to exist. Most of us have been brought up on the streets. Our way has been to steal and kill and destroy the wealthy, and we do the same amongst our own when they are a threat. We have known no other way," he explained, as he looked around at his people. "We practise an eye for an eye and a tooth for a tooth. Now I'm telling you something new. If they come and punch you in the face, don't retaliate. Offer your other cheek."

A great cheer went up as his people listened. They laughed and leaned over and playfully punched each other.

"I have shared with you God's commandments. I want to explain to you these commandments embrace two main principles. It is this: the first half is about your love to God, and the second half is about your love for others, and that means the wealthy out there as well. We must return warmth from their coldness.

"Remember how I told you Jesus loves you just as you are? You are a pearl of great price to Him. Well, I want to tell you something new. He has a special work for you in this city. Terrible times are coming upon Sydney. Countless people will die. He will have His people, and they will be recognised by their love for each other and for their enemies.

"This reminds me, you can't love two masters. You can't follow spirit mediums from demons and serve God at the same time. You must give your lives to Jesus and keep His commandment of love. Do this, and God will be with you when the great devastation comes upon this earth."

## Chapter 26

# Mobile Homes

Robert and Julie were staying at Grandma Johnston's property near Bathurst. They were thankful they'd moved when Robert found out about Albert and the secret Jesuits and sad when they heard what happened to him and Janet. Most of all, they were very concerned when they heard Anita was missing.

Sitting on Grandma Johnston's wide veranda that commanded views across a distant paddock, they discussed this problem.

Grandma Johnston watched the children quietly approach and listen unnoticed to the adults' conversation.

"Children, run along and feed the chickens, and don't forget to collect the eggs," she reminded them.

The children pushed and shoved and laughed as they called to each other. They ran to the chickens that pecked freely in the garden. Their family was one of the lucky ones, as they had a regular trickle of water from their bore.

"We are so worried about Janet's daughter, Anita," explained Julie to her mother. "We keep looking for her when we're on the road. There are reports of so many terrible things happening out there, especially to young girls."

"Well, all you can do is pray, dear, and keep looking," Grandma Johnston said.

"Mum, you should see the people out there. With COVID-19 and the closing of shops and businesses, and with the stimulus packages now finished, the banks are foreclosing on many peoples' loans. There are homeless people everywhere." She sighed. "Anita may have been helped by one of them." She gazed sadly across the dry paddocks.

Robert continued. "People couldn't travel or leave their districts when the virus was in full swing, but now with no new cases in Australia, we are free to move around, but still not for travel overseas. People who have any type of camping gear or those with caravans and motor homes have set up camp in designated free sites. These spots are only meant for a day or two, but people are camping there for weeks, especially if there's water. The police are regularly checking the sites and keeping the numbers down."

"Did I tell you?" Grandma Johnston said. "Two men from the social security department visited me and told me that people owning properties, or have spare bedrooms in their homes, are expected to house the unemployed. Many in the cities are housed in disused motels that the government has confiscated. The rooms are free, and they have stamps to buy food. Crime is at an all-time high in the cities, and because of this, we are now experiencing a mobile population."

***Two men from the social security department visited me and told me that people owning properties, or have spare bedrooms in their homes, are expected to house the unemployed.***

"Yes, it's too dangerous for them to return to the cities. It's good for witnessing, though," Julie replied. "Having them all together gives us a chance to help many at one stop." She smiled, and her cheerful self surfaced for a moment.

Robert joined in. "I think we should go back on the road and keep on witnessing and helping those in need before it's too late."

"Mum, could you please take care of the children for a few weeks?"

"Of course, dear," answered Grandma Johnston.

Julie stood, "I'll pack the motorhome immediately."

* * *

Robert and Julie drove past farming properties. Drought conditions were evident in the paddocks with yellow stubble and creeks with only muddy puddles, or they were completely dry. Dam walls were cracked with hardened mud. The cattle had long been shot.

Young men on foot with large packs travelled the road in search of seasonal work that was in short supply or non-existent. These young men were desperate for work because of government cuts in welfare funds.

They reminded Julie of stories her grandma had told about swagmen in the Great Depression between the two world wars. They would come to farms looking for work and food.

Her grandma would always say, "You need a good war to clear the economy," and Julie wondered if that would happen again.

Soon, Robert and Julie stopped at Balranald and prepared leaflets and other materials for posting. These were to go to homes in that area through the Australian Postal service. They felt it was their duty to warn the citizens of Australia of the coming events. They had already mailed over thirty thousand leaflets and books across Australia's inland stations.

"A man at the post office told me we're wasting our money and time posting out this material because people dump so-called junk mail. What do you think, Jules?" Robert asked.

"God's Word won't return to us void. Robert, when are you going to learn the Lord will take care of His business and people will read these magazines and books? Have some faith, doubting Thomas," she teased.

The next morning, Julie spoke to God, telling Him about Robert's need for reassurance. "Perhaps, Lord, give him some type of confirmation," she prayed.

On their way back to camp they saw a young fellow. He walked along the road with a heavy backpack. Robert stopped. "Hi! Mate, need a lift?"

He opened the side door and let the young man in. Julie gave up her front seat and sat at the table. The hitch-hiker looked like a stockman. He wore jeans, leather boots, and a checked shirt. A felt hat was pulled down over his eyes. He carried something in a long, narrow cloth bag, as well as his pack.

"People don't pick me up when I'm carrying this," he indicated at the cloth bag. "They think I'm carrying a gun, but it isn't. It's a whip, that's all." Looking at them he asked, "What made you pick me up?"

Julie walked to the front of the van, holding a book behind her back. She leaned forward and placed the book in his hands. She was well pleased with herself and grinned broadly.

"We're posting out books, and we'd like to give you this one." It was *The Great Controversy*.

The young chap looked at the book and laughed. "I'm a stockman from a station near Alice Springs. Oh, by the way, my name is Joss," he said and continued. "The boss received this very book in his mailbox with others in a parcel. They placed the books in our bunkhouse. I'm reading this one right now. It's in my pack," and he nodded to his pack on his lap. "You know, I've been thinking about it constantly."

Julie had prayed that morning, and it was only mid-afternoon, and God had already answered her prayer. She looked up and smirked at Robert, raising her eyebrows as if to say, "*See, doubting Thomas!*" She went back to her seat and quietly prayed under her breath, "Thank You, Lord, for confirming that the books are being read."

At the free campsite, there were at least twenty others. All seemed to be escaping the cities. They had crowded into a small paddock near a very muddy dam.

The police were knocking on the campers' doors. "You must be tested for the virus, and remember, social distancing is still law," they explained, as they placed virus 19 test swabs into their mouths. Other cops were busy writing down their information and results.

Julie noticed a girl with a small baby that was crying lustily. *I wonder what's wrong with her baby,* she thought. She walked over to see if she could help. *The mother's only a child, and she, too, has been crying for some time by the look of her swollen eyes.*

Her heart went out to the girl. "Hello, my name is Julie. Can I help, dear? What's the matter with your baby?"

"Cooper's hungry," the girl sniffed. "I think my milk is drying up. I've cut back on my bottled water, as I'm nearly out." She wiped her nose and continued. "Mum said I must drink plenty to make enough milk. They've been held up and won't be here for another two days. I'm stranded." She sobbed deeply. "I must make my water last, as the water here is undrinkable." She continued to weep and wipe her face with her sleeve. She looked down at her son and gently touched his cheek. He swung his little head with his mouth wide open, trying to grab at something in the hope it might be nourishment. The girl lifted the little bundle to her shoulder and rocked him gently.

"Well, I can help you," said Julie. "We have plenty of water. Come with me to our bus." She walked to the back of the bus and opened the boot. "Here, take these bottles of water and some canned food. See? We have plenty."

"Thank you, but are you sure?"

Julie nodded and walked back to the girl's tent with the supplies. *Thank You, Lord, for these supplies, but, Lord, there is so many hungry people, and what we have will soon be depleted. Please help us to provide more,* Julie silently prayed as she walked back to her bus.

That evening, the young chap, Joss, made camp at their site. Around the campfire they had an opportunity to share with him the events in the book *The Great Controversy* that he was reading. With torches in hand, they read with him portions from their Bibles.

The next morning, they prayed for God's guidance and protection for everything that might transpire through the day.

Robert and Julie gave Joss a lift to town. At the roadhouse he managed to obtain a ride with a truck driver.

## Chapter 27

# Outreach

Robert and Julie went to the post office to continue with their mail-out. Robert went to a wall of metal boxes and located his. He unlocked it and sat down on a low wall opposite to read his mail. Julie went into the office with her heavy cardboard box containing more than twenty envelopes filled with leaflets and books.

"I'm sorry, but there are insufficient funds in this account," said the lass trying to access Julie's card.

"We've been posting huge amounts, but I was sure we still had some funds," Julie replied, embarrassed.

Just then, the postmaster entered the room and asked if he could help.

"Oh, I've got carried away and used all our funds, that's all," Julie laughed self-consciously.

"Well, let me take this box of mail and process it for you," said the postmaster without a smile. "It's on the house, seeing you've placed so much work through here."

"Thank you," Julie grinned.

The postmaster looked up, nodded, and smiled.

*Thank You, God. Not once have You let us down*, she thought.

When outside, Julie found her husband. "Robert, have a guess what the Lord has done for us," she laughed. While she excitedly told him what had happened, she realised he had a smug expression on his face. He, too, had a surprise.

Robert took a deep breath. "Now, let me tell you about this letter I'm holding. You know how we placed our house on the market so we could witness? Well, I have a letter from the real estate agent. There's an offer on our home and a signed contract with a deposit of ten thousand dollars; it is at the real estate office. They'll swap our property for their unit in the centre of Sydney, and also a very isolated block in the Blue Mountains. All of this for our place." He sounded very surprised. "This is really a miracle. Our house is new, but it's only on two hectares in the outer suburbs."

"Praise the Lord! Two miracles in one day and we mustn't forget our answer to prayer yesterday," Julie said.

Robert looked concerned. "I'm not sure what to think about accepting a unit in the city. Perhaps we should ask for more money and turn down the unit."

"Robert, how could you!" Julie said horrified. "Ye of little faith; you know we promised to leave it in the Lord's hands. He knows what's best. It's perfect because God has organised this sale and so quickly and at such a bad time in the economy. We must accept it, Robert. God knows what's best. I'm sure He has a plan."

"We'll have to sign a contract in the next two days for the sale to go through. We need to go immediately," Robert answered.

They headed straight back to Sydney. About an hour later, they came around a corner and ran into a police roadblock.

"Sorry, folk, but you'll have to go back the way you came. There are terrible bushfires ahead."

"Isn't there somewhere we can cut through?" Robert asked. "We're getting low on fuel."

"Sorry, mate, it's not safe, but there's a fuel station about fifty kilometres back," answered the officer, eyeing Robert with suspicion.

Robert knew not to push it, as people were being arrested as terrorists for the slightest thing. He didn't want the police looking at his fuel gauge, as it showed quarter full, and the cop might become even more suspicious. After all, who in their right mind would travel without fuel or money, with raging bushfires threatening most of the state? He thought. *I can't see how we can make it now, which means the contract won't go through, and what are we going to do without money?*

Robert knew he couldn't ring Grandma Johnston, as her phone had been disconnected, and she didn't own a mobile phone. He didn't say a word to Julie, who stared out the window at barren paddocks.

Taking a detour, they drove their motor home for another 100 kilometres, and then it started to splutter and jerk. Finally, it stalled. It started up again, spluttered, drove for a few metres, jerked, and stopped. Julie looked at the petrol gauge; it showed empty. The red light had been on for many kilometres.

"God can get us there, Robert. Let's pray."

They went to the back of their van and knelt. Robert felt despondent as he thought of their plight. "Dear heavenly Father, time is short, and money soon won't be of any use to us," he prayed. "We must learn to rely on You for all our needs. We need to get to Sydney, and our bus is out of fuel, and we don't have money to get more. If it's Your will for us to sign this contract, please start this bus and let Your angels push it to its destination. We pray this in Your Son Jesus' lovely name, and we thank You for the help You are about to give us. Amen."

They climbed back into their seats and buckled their seatbelts. Robert started the bus. The motor turned over and purred down the road. Later, they pulled up at their destination, still with an empty fuel tank that had been empty for the last two hundred kilometres.

They thanked the Lord for His great mercy, and Robert signed the contract, knowing it was God's will.

## Chapter 28

# Hidden Mountain Retreat

Julie and Robert visited their lawyer and completed the transaction of sale. Driving through Sydney, they watched people in the city's main thoroughfare. Shops that had been closed for six months because of the virus were now opened. The streets, once empty, now had cars driving on the busy thoroughfare. People were trying to get on with their lives.

When they arrived home, they collapsed in their lounge room, glad to be home. They listened to Australia Broadcasting Live News.

Max Hiller was reporting on recent developments. "Several countries still haven't signed the United Nations treaty, which creates ten international zones for commerce and trade. A spokesman has stated that these nations will soon feel the blight of not being part of the world trade arrangements."

Max Hiller turned to the next camera. "China has become the world's leading nation in trade and has signed an agreement with the One World Government. She has instituted a state-run church for her people with a Sunday rest day for all citizens. Missionaries working outside these state churches have been discouraged and even shot. China's leaders say that they have long recognised the importance of a united world in trade and are willing to lead the way in showing the value of the United Nations initiative. For this reason, China is willing to follow all the One World Government laws."

The Australian Prime Minister appeared on the TV screen. "In four weeks, the international monetary funds through the government will finance all other banks and societies. Do not worry, as this will be accomplished automatically. Your current bank will operate but as a subsidiary of the World Bank. But please remember, you must be correctly identified with the One World ID card to buy or sell, to hold a job, and school your children. People who do not obey these orders will not be tolerated. If you sympathise with these people and help them or employ them in trade, your actions will be treated as treason. You will be imprisoned without question."

Julie and Robert looked at each other, shocked. They understood from their Bible studies that these things would happen, but not so soon.

Robert looked pale as he sat thinking. “I believe that people will be forced to sign forms of allegiance to the United Nations and the Sunday laws. At first, they will bring in a Sunday rest day for the health of the planet. Because of the virus, last year’s world-wide lockdown showed that the planet’s pollution improved. Now they want a lockdown for the world every Sunday. Eventually, we will be expected to attend the state church, which will be used as the platform for the government to deliver its propaganda programs. They’ll conduct headcounts of the enrolled congregations. We are going to be forced to sell our souls for a bowl of stew, like Esau in the Bible.”

“Yes, we must make the money we have received from our house count for God’s work, as we won’t join them. We must stay loyal to God,” answered Julie. She looked around her lounge room. “I think we should sell all our furniture and knick-knacks as quickly as we can. We should buy a pile of foam mattresses, for the unit and the mountain property. I believe there’ll be many believers sheltering at both places.”

Robert nodded. “Yes, and the rest of the money must go on food. We can store cans and suchlike for God’s homeless at these places. Oh! And we mustn’t forget fuel,” he added with a sheepish grin. “Jules, we mustn’t under any circumstances give out our addresses. I don’t know how long we’ll get away with it because surely the government will check who holds registered titles, and what will happen when we have to pay the council rates? And how will we let people know they can use these places?’

“The same way we must do everything from now on,” Julie sighed. “Through faith and faith alone. This is God’s business, so He will take care of it. We’ll leave the doors closed but not locked on both properties. God will bring those who belong to Him that need shelter and food. The others won’t come. I know that He will put a protective hand over the titles of these properties. I feel we should pray, don’t you?”

Both knelt with thankful hearts and minds determined to serve God, no matter what might happen.

They had one week before the new owners took over the house. Robert borrowed a trailer from his neighbour, and they cleaned and scrubbed the house and tossed and tossed some more. Julie was surprised how in the past, they had collected useless things. Toward the end of the week, a second-hand dealer came with his truck to collect their goods.

When they were paid at the settlement of the sale, they quickly went to a large department store and filled the trailer with thick foam mattresses. They left them on their empty lounge room floor and went off again to buy quilts, quilt covers, pillows and pillowcases, towels, and other linen.

"It feels like Christmas," said Julie, laughing as they dragged the goods into their house. They were taking all the goods to their city unit.

"Let's go and see our unit," Robert said.

They drove to Surry Hills, near Paddington. The terrace unit was a two-story one-hundred-year-old building. It stood on the corner of a quiet street lined with similar buildings, standing there in all their historic grandeur. It had a white lacy iron balustrade on its upper balcony. It seemed well presented, with painted blue walls, white window frames, and a stained timber front door. The neighbouring building attached to theirs had a high painted brick wall dividing their front verandas.

There was a small cottage garden at the front, and the yard was well fenced. At the back of the property was a single garage with doors opening onto a side lane. The back yard had a lawn with a rotary clothesline in the middle. Behind the shed was a flat, wide tank without a top, lying on its side.

"I wonder what they were going to do with this tank," Robert said.

"I don't know," Julie answered. "But I do know one thing; we have been given a very expensive property. In good times, it would cost millions to buy. It's dangerous in the city, and this is possibly the reason they've offloaded it. I can't wait to see our mountain block."

They placed all the things they had brought from their home into their unit and then unpacked the food supply, realising that soon, very soon, they wouldn't be able to buy or sell anything.

* * *

Julie and Robert left two days before the new owners took ownership of their home in the outskirts of Sydney. Behind their motorhome, they pulled the trailer purchased from their neighbour, laden with boxes of food, cans of diesel, tools, and bedding, linen, clothes, crockery, cutlery, pots, and pans—some new, and some from their sold home.

The vehicle crawled up the mountains on the Great Western Highway, turning into Blue Mountain Road near Katoomba. It was bitumen at first but then petered out to a narrow dirt road. After bumping along for some time, they noticed a weed-covered track with a sign that said "Private Property. Keep Out."

"The map says this is where we turn," Julie said. "See the fish? They said on the bottom of the sign was a small drawing of a fish. I think the original owners must be Christians!"

Robert drove very slowly down the overgrown track. Soon they came to a grassy clearing where they noticed a large iron shed on a riverbank.

Excitedly, they climbed out of the van and looked around. Above them on all sides were majestic mountains that formed their own small valley.

They walked to the edge of the river, which was obviously very low because of the drought. The stones in the riverbed jutted up, and water meandered around them. Tall gums and willows flanked the high banks, and tall shady trees hung over part of the shed.

Robert jangled the keys and unlocked the shed's only door. Inside there was a cement floor and no lining on the walls, but all windows were screened, which was a good thing. About halfway along the wall was a wood stove for cooking and a sink connected to a large rainwater tank outside.

"Robert, I think we should divide both ends into male and female dormitories. We could build female and male showers with pit toilets outside. We also need bunks and a large table with chairs for the kitchen."

"Tomorrow, we'll go into town with the trailer and buy materials," Robert said. "I think I can divide the shed and build the bunks easily enough, and the showers and toilets won't take long." He thought to himself, *Julie never stops organising and setting up house. A natural optimist, that's for sure.*

The next morning, they woke early to a chorus of birds. They stood by their van in awe at mist-covered mountaintops. The air felt clean and fresh.

"Let's walk upriver on the rocks," Robert said with a big smile. "It's early, and if we walk for half an hour, we should be back in plenty of time to go to town."

As they jumped from rock to rock, they marvelled at God's great love. "The children will love this place," Julie laughed. "I can't wait to bring them here."

"What a perfect hidden valley!" Robert called back, and there it was: a waterfall— or what was a waterfall when the river was flowing. It was now a small stream to the right of a wide, dry cave. The rocks underfoot allowed them to enter the cave, and they walked around on dry ground.

"Oh no!" Julie squealed as a flurry of wings swirled about her head. "What are they?" she yelled with her face hidden in her folded arms.

"Black bats; they're settling now. They're hanging from the roof. Look up," Robert teased, "and you'll see them."

"No way!" she yelled over the racket and scurried away from the squealing, noisy little vampires.

Four weeks later, with the building alterations completed, they travelled back to their children.

"What's happening, Robert?" Julie asked, pointing. "Look at all those people."

"When I was in the shops collecting our supplies, I heard people speak about it," Robert replied. "People are saying that when the government's international monetary funds take over the banks, everyone's accounts will have equal monetary value. So, people are cancelling their shares in the stock exchange, and buying gold, or cashing their super-funds, and others are removing their cash and buying commodities like we did. Some are even paying out their mortgages and personal debts. They have been told the government will take ownership of unpaid properties and goods."

"Won't all of this bring on a crash?" Julie asked.

Robert paused for a moment and considered. "It's all different from past depression days. The banks will close. I am surprised it hasn't happened already, and then they will open and follow immediately with their new program."

They returned to Grandma's farm and shared their news. The children were excited that their parents were spending Christmas with them. They were all, including Grandma, going to their new retreat, Shangri-La.

# Chapter 29

# Jerusalem

It was midnight, and black-cloaked men, their faces shielded by hoods, slowly wound down a narrow path near the Damascus Gate in Jerusalem. They walked to the ancient stoneworks known to some as the Royal Quarries. White stone from these quarries had been used many centuries ago to build Solomon's temple.

Freemasons from all parts of the world held lodge meetings at night in the quarry caverns. Deep in the bowels of the earth, they were neither disturbed nor observed. All held to the theory that the builders of Solomon's temple were Freemasons.

Who were the unknown men entering the cavern? These men of high official rank, higher than members of all the secret societies, now entered one by one.

Brad and Steven stood outside the quarries with their machine guns, ready for action. They were working as guards and agents for the CIA there to protect these men of high official rank.

In the cavern, candles flickered in many small wall recesses. They glowed with a burnished light against the white stone. At the back was a table, covered with a royal blue silk cloth with gold stars and moon emblems. Behind was a large chair like a throne. Five more ornate chairs stood on each side. A wide semicircle of tables and chairs, covered with the same cloth, were arranged in front of the main table. All held jugs of water and drinking glasses.

***Standing at their post, Brad and Steven gasped as they watched. It was Pope Nicholas.***

The cloaked men entered and stood behind their chairs in the semicircle. They were the officials of Jerusalem and cardinals from the ten regions of the world. The men who followed were Thirty-Third-Degree Masons. These were the secret rulers of the world; they stood behind the chairs at the front, five on each side of the main chair. Then the last hooded person, whom Brad and Steven accompanied to the door, entered and stood in front of the throne chair. He took off his cloak, and they all followed. Standing at their post, Brad and Steven gasped as they watched. It was Pope Nicholas.

The officials stood in front of their pontiff with heads bowed. He lifted his arms and blessed them, and then he prayed. He sat and indicated for them to follow.

Pope Nicholas spoke. "For the past two weeks, I have been with the United Nations Secretary General and the leaders of the ten world zones. The Israel Minister of Justice, now backs a two-day weekend, thus honouring Sunday as a rest day and closure for business. Trade and Industry Board Members of Argentina support the Sunday Rest Bill. European Trade Union Confederation has agreed to pass a Sunday law in Europe. Most countries have signed the agreement to implement the New World program. There are a few countries still considering its implications. I'm sure when they sit down with their parliaments and discuss the issues, they will realise the great benefits. It's important for them to join the United Nations at this difficult time. If they don't join, the consequences for their country will be great. Help will be withdrawn from them in trade, defence, education, travel, health, and communications. Without the United Nations, peace will elude them and financial depression and civil riots will take over their country. Yes, the people of the world must realise that they should unite for peace and for the prosperity of mankind. It is the only way to save this planet."

Pope Nicholas continued. "The Islamic terrorist attacks are instigated by bigotry from religious extremists. This must stop. We need world peace and unity. We have spent many days and nights discussing this matter in the United Nations meetings. The Protestant Christian Coalition in America agrees. It says the One World Church with all its different facets of religion, is the only way to bring unity and peace to the world. This will give it a united voice for all mankind."

He looked around at his cardinals and the leaders of Jerusalem. "We all realize that the Middle East stands in the way of real progress. There will be, of course, other dissenters. We'll deal with these people through the terrorist laws that are now in place internationally, but our real concern is the problems in this region. We need religious peace between the Muslims and the Jews. They have been fighting since the time of Abraham, and it must stop—now."

After a dramatic pause, he continued. "Israel has agreed to the Vatican gaining sovereignty over Jerusalem and the Temple Mount. The city will become the capital of Israel, but will be administrated by the Vatican."

After a short discussion with the leaders of Israel, all could see the benefits of political and religious control by the United Nations and the Vatican. It would give Jerusalem protection. The documents were brought forward and signed.

"We have a surprise for you tonight," Pope Nicholas said. "This evening I am going to expose the Holy Grail. This is the true Holy Grail. Not the many different ones that have been written about over centuries, and not the latest that churches have been arguing about. The latest tale is about ten stone coffins that have been unearthed by an archaeologist in a suburb of Jerusalem. They say they once held bones of Jesus, his parents Mary and Joseph, his wife Mary, and their son Judah. We are happy for people to be confused by this tale; it suits our purpose. It will take their eyes off our project. We are happy that famous film producers and novel writers have written stories about this so-called find by the archaeologist.

"Now, I want you to know about the true Holy Grail. It is our secret, and the world must not be told until we have it safely in our hands. The Holy Grail is the famous ark of the covenant that was housed in Solomon's temple. We believe it is hidden in a mysterious underground passage linked to these quarries. We have been given permission by the Israeli Government's Head of Antiquities to excavate this great treasure.

"It's important for the papacy and Israel to own this wonderful artefact, and to have it grace our new temple in Jerusalem. We realise that to own the ark will bring together Jews, Christians, and Muslims, who at the moment, make up an explosive cocktail! This is the means to bring peace on earth!" Pope Nicholas said, very much pleased with his news.

His audience was excited and burst into a frenzy of clapping and talking. Pope Nicholas let them continue for a few minutes, and then clapped his hands, and waiters brought in the banquet. Relaxed, they ate and drank the best food and wine in Israel and talked about the wonderful future they all would have in the New Jerusalem.

## Chapter 30

# Ten World Zones

Several weeks later, official cars with their delegates from the ten world zones stopped at Jerusalem's Government House. They were followed by the General of the United Nations Peace Corps, who was stationed in Jerusalem. It was important for him to attend, as his army was needed to keep peace in Israel and on its borders.

Visitors and locals stopped to watch the important world delegates enter the foyer of Government House dressed in colourful national dress and headgear. These people were ushered into the boardroom past Steven and Brad on guard duty.

Soon, several other official cars pulled up to the kerb. From the lead car, Pope Nicholas alighted. He entered with his Vatican officials and bodyguards. All watching drew in their breaths. Many crossed themselves, and others bowed their heads. Soon, all had entered the boardroom. Brad and Steven closed the doors and stood outside, holding their automatic machine guns to their chests.

All delegates sat, but Pope Nicholas stood and leaned over a model centred on a large table and smiled. He seemed very pleased with what he was going to present.

"This is a model of Jerusalem. See? This is the wall that surrounds the city." He pointed with a special stick. "Now, here's the Holy Sepulchre, and over here is the Dome of the Rock." He pointed out other important sites in the city.

"We have spent a lot of time discussing the Dome of the Rock. It is positioned on the site where Solomon's temple was built." He cleared his throat and looked around. "We wish to build a replica of Solomon's temple, with the holy ark of the covenant gracing the temple's Most Holy Place. We feel that it should be built in the vicinity of the original temple. It would cause unnecessary strife if we interfered with the Dome." He took a deep breath, straightened, and quickly continued. "So! This is our plan. The temple will be built as a museum of the past and will be placed at the far end of beautiful gardens. There will be special areas for services for Jews, Christians, and Muslims. Also, all the other groups in the different world cultures. After all, we are now united under one banner." The pope walked to his chair and sat. He was glad his speech was over, but he wasn't sure how the Islamic leaders would take the news.

The architect stood and showed an individual model of the museum in the gardens. "You can see the museum will be built the same as Solomon's temple. It will be plain and oblong and made of sandstone from the quarries. See here; these are two high brass pillars on each side of the extremely large front doors." He showed drawings of the building's interior. See, here we will place the ark of the covenant. Instead of a heavy veil as they had in the original, we will have a bullet-proof wall."

Next, he showed the gardens. "These gardens will resemble, as far as possible, the Garden of Eden."

None present could dispute what they saw, and all seemed well pleased with Pope Nicholas' presentation. They retired to the dining hall to a sumptuous dinner with champagne to continue their discussions.

Brad and Steven accompanied the Vatican staff while they removed the model. The staff repeated in English the exciting but very confidential news. "You mustn't repeat what you've heard," they said, with fingers to their lips.

The boys retired to the staff dining area. They were shocked, to say the least, with the unfolding events.

"Well, mate, it looks as if Pope Nicholas will be Vicar of Christ over the One World Church," Brad said. "What do you think about that? You have more knowledge than me."

"I'm shocked," Steven answered. "Did you hear what they said about special services in Solomon's temple? It blew me away. Fancy them using the same set-up as in the past."

Brad grinned. "Mate, it's brilliant. On the Day of Atonement, a lamb would be placed on the altar in the outer court—after all, it's a museum—and they'll act out the old ceremonial service. Then, at the appropriate time, the head priest himself—I reckon that'll be the Pope—will stand in front of the ark of the covenant and offer up the people's sins that have been confessed to him. They'll offer their sins with the lamb's blood and incense," Brad said, not realising the implications of what he had just described.

Steven shook his head at his friend. "I wonder if they'll go to the other side of the bullet-proof partition to offer up their sins. In the past, if they passed the veil and were not anointed, they were slain by God's power there." He frowned and continued. "I wonder what the Jews and Muslims think?"

"Well, the Jews should be pleased," Brad answered.

"It's alarming!" Steven exclaimed. "It makes no sense, using the sanctuary. In the old service, the lamb sacrifice pointed to Jesus shedding His blood on the cross for their sins. They forget that it's been fulfilled. Jesus has risen from the grave and now mediates in the heavenly sanctuary for you and me. What they are about to do will do away with the truth."

# Chapter 31

# Prisoners of the State

In the meantime, Sister Maria and the other nuns were still held as prisoners of the State. They had been removed from the cells just after Albert's death, but they were still in the convent in the mountains west of Sydney.

The convent had changed after Albert's death. The Islamic women were now in family groups on the first floor; they had been held in the convent for over a year while they waited patiently for transportation overseas.

Sister Maria entered the kitchen. The new group of Islamic women working there looked up and smiled. "They seem happy enough," she remarked to a junior nun accompanying her.

The nun nodded and looked outside where women worked in the gardens, tending vegetables for the table. "Yes," she answered, "they realise the State is helping them. They're happy to be here, especially after what the citizens have put them through—who would want to be in the city at the moment with the restrictions the government is placing on the population?" she said with a shudder and moved aside as Sister Maria stepped into the courtyard.

"Yes, I've been told most people have left the cities for quiet places in the country," Sister Maria answered. "Many are living like gypsies. They're living in caravans, mobile homes, tents ..." She sighed and shook her head. "I suppose they are happy that they moved out in time, in case the cities and country regions become locked down for a second time with the COVID-19. I believe it is still raging overseas."

"Yes, and many are without food," her companion added.

Sister Maria absent-mindedly pulled a flower as she walked. "It must be very dangerous out there with so many desperate people on the road." She muttered, more to herself than anybody else, "I must visit Frank."

"Sister Maria! Sister Maria!" children called as they came running across the courtyard. "Sister Maria, the Mary statue spoke to us. We were sitting on the seat in front of her. We heard stories how she had spoken before, so we prayed to her, and she spoke to us! She said we all had to unite with the One World Government for peace. She said we had to belong to its church, and if we do this, God will heal the environment. Is that right, Sister Maria?" They looked up at her eagerly.

Sister Maria sighed heavily. Once, she would have agreed with them. She once believed the miracles of Fatima. Now she knew better. How was she going to answer their questions? "Tonight, we will have a study on the error of immortality of the soul. We will announce the time at the dinner table. Now, go along, children, and play. The convent is filled with legions of evil angels," she said to the other nun when the children were safely out of earshot. "We must pray for the covering protection of God's angels when we present this topic tonight."

"Well, that's if they come," answered the other nun. "Remember, they're Muslims, and their beliefs are different from ours."

But that evening, all families were present. Apparently, some of the adults had witnessed Mary's apparition as well. They were scared and wanted answers. Sister Maria prayed and used her Bible to prove that Mary was still in her grave and couldn't talk with them.

When the meeting finished, it was late, and Sister Maria was exhausted, but she felt she should look in on Father Frank. She'd heard he was failing fast. She entered the cell without a mask or gown and sat quietly next to his bed. He was connected to tubes for survival. His breath was shallow, and she feared it might be too late to speak with him. She lowered her head and sought the Lord in prayer.

Father Frank opened his eyes. The room was filled with light. He blinked and saw celestial beings of radiant light everywhere in the room. Near Sister Maria was a tall angel with wings that folded around her.

Frank knew there was another world within this world, another dimension of created beings. Some were angels that came back and forth from heaven, and some were demons that were fallen angels who now ruled this earth. Most people weren't aware of them and couldn't see them, although there were those who liked to tell others they were in touch with the dead. Satan gloated as he used these "spirit mediums" to give his message. He enabled them to predict the future and perform miracles and healings.

Father Frank knew better, as he had studied scripture that clearly told him the dead slept and knew nothing. It also told him that the dead in Christ would be resurrected at Jesus' second coming, but he was forbidden to teach this. He had lost his spiritual walk with the Lord because he compromised the truth with doctrines of man.

Sister Maria noticed he was awake. “Frank, I’ve come to pray with you.”

“I’m lost. It’s too late,” he mumbled.

“God loves you, Frank, and is waiting for you to pray and confess your sins. You don’t need a priest; Jesus is your high priest in the heavenly sanctuary, and He’s waiting to hear from you,” she said as she held his hands.

Frank knew this from his childhood; he was close to God back then. He nodded and slowly, in an inaudible whisper, prayed to the Lord. His face relaxed, and for the first time, she saw peace on his countenance; then, he died.

# Chapter 32

# Proscribed

Pat and Eddy had been visiting Pat's mother in Adelaide. Her doctor had arranged for tests by the Aged Care Assessment Team. Dementia was diagnosed, and the family had to make arrangements for a nursing home. When Pat's mother realised this, she became very cross.

"You're no daughter of mine," she snarled. "If you were, you wouldn't be putting me away." She dropped her head and muttered, "I know you. You've planned all of this. You're wicked."

"Mum, your doctor ordered the test," Pat answered. Then kindlier, "Sweetie, I'm sorry, but it's not as bad as it seems. You'll see."

Pat's mother was taken to the Bay Park Nursing Home. She had a lovely private room looking over the gardens. Grumbling all the while, she reluctantly settled into her new room and routine.

A busy time followed as they cleaned and cleared the home so it could be placed on the market. Eddy spent many days in the gardens, which were overgrown and much neglected. They then spent a few weeks visiting family and friends.

"Eddy, before we go home, let's once again visit Mum," Pat suggested.

When they arrived, the entrance gate was locked, and a large sign explained the lockdown procedures. They hadn't been listening to the news and weren't aware of a new outbreak of COVID-19. The old restrictions were now back in place.

"This is terrible," Pat exclaimed. "Mum will be terrified." She thought for a moment. "Her room has a large window overlooking the gardens; maybe we can catch her there and wave goodbye."

They walked around the corner and peered through a tall fence, and there she was with head down, sleeping in her chair. Pat retrieved the phone from her bag and rang. They could see her mother reaching and answering her phone on the locker. "Mum, look up; we are outside your window," Pat spoke loudly.

Still, with head down, she answered. "What are you doing at my window? You should be in my room, not at a window," she grumbled.

"Mum, just stand up and go to your window," explained Pat.

She did, and they waved madly. At first, she waved back, and then shook her head and went back to her chair, dropping her head once again.

"She doesn't understand," Pat said wiping tears away.

"She'll be fine," replied Eddy. "Mum has the family to visit her, and I am sure the home will try and explain what is happening."

As they passed through different districts, they noticed the streets were once again nearly empty. Police were everywhere. People were being fined on the spot for not keeping to the restriction of numbers. High-rise tenement units held bored people. Some were staring through windows. Others were leaning over their balconies, watching mask-wearing people pass by. Masked people protecting themselves from other masked people. All walked on quickly, not speaking or approaching each other. Then, they noticed people crowding into banks or queuing down the streets, waiting to enter.

* * *

At the airport, they were shocked to see lots of police and army personnel. Soon, they were made aware of what was happening.

"Please line up here," a police officer explained to the group travelling to Sydney. "Yes, you two must line up as well," he gruffly explained to Pat and Eddy.

People were showing papers, or their cell phones, to police sitting at desks. The army men were directing the crowd or just standing around in a menacing fashion.

"I think we were supposed to fill in forms of some sort," whispered Eddy. Eddy moved ahead to a cop at the end of the table. There didn't seem to be any problems.

"Next," called a cop, and it was Pat's turn. "Have you filled in your travel permit papers? You were supposed to download them from your computer or to use your cell phone when you booked your flight," he explained.

"I didn't know," explained Pat. "We booked ages ago, and we don't have a computer."

"Well, let's go through the papers together," he explained. "Have you had the COVID-19 virus? Have you been in a virus hot spot? Do you have a cough or fever? Do you feel unwell? Have you been tested recently for the virus?" The questions continued, and the forms were ticked. "Next time you travel, it will be worse. You will be expected to have all this information and your COVID-19 vaccination certificate on your cell phone," he said, not unkindly.

On the plane back to Sydney, Pat nudged Eddy. "I don't think we've listened to the news once while away. We've been so busy, but I'm glad Mum's safe. Eddy, did you hear what I said? I'm glad Mum's safe," she repeated, but Eddy, exhausted, was fast asleep.

They arrived at Sydney, and, being summer, it was still light. Eddy stumbled toward the train still half asleep.

"It's good of Julie and Robert to lend us their unit," Pat said, as they entered the train and sat. "It's close to the city centre, which will be a good thing for us."

"The district is called Surry Hills," Eddy corrected.

"We have so much to attend to tomorrow. It's going to be a really busy day," Pat said, looking at her husband. She thought to herself as she looked at his dishevelled appearance. *I must keep an eye on Eddy; he doesn't look well.*

"I'm really pleased we kept these seasonal passes," she continued when the conductor passed.

Dismounting at their stop, they dragged their cases a few streets to Surry Hills.

"What a lovely unit," Pat said, as they stood in front of the heritage townhouse. "What a blessing that Julie and Robert have made it available for others."

"I wonder where the key's kept," Eddy said.

"Don't worry; the door will be shut, but not locked. They said the unit belongs to God, and He will take care of it," Pat answered.

They entered, noticing mattresses piled in the corner of the lounge room. They looked in the cupboards and found food and other supplies.

"I think," Pat suggested, "We should go to the shops and buy our food and leave these supplies for others less fortunate."

They went down the street toward the highway, passing a block of department stores. They noticed a Woolworth's sign, went in, and collected a few items. When finished, they pushed their groceries through the register and produced cash.

"Sorry, but we don't use cash anymore," the assistant said.

They reached for their cards. The lass looked bored.

"Sorry, we don't use those bankcards anymore. Don't you realize the One World ID card has been issued to all citizens? Everybody received their cards last month. Do you have your cell phone?" she asked, as she turned a screen towards Pat. "You can use your phone to buy groceries," she explained. "Just hold it to the screen, and all your details will come up."

"I didn't know that," replied Pat, as she retrieved the phone from her bag. "Our son has given us this phone. It is new, you know, and he has entered different apps, but I haven't checked them as yet."

The girl nodded. She took the cell phone and held it to the screen. Pat's banking page displayed a foreclosure of her account.

"We've been away," Pat said, embarrassed. "Can we leave these things with you?" she asked and took the phone back. They quickly walked out of the shop, not realising the police now had all her contact details, photo, and also the foreclosure of her account. This would immediately alert them of terrorist intentions.

They hurried back to the unit. This time, they took a side street and noticed people throwing books into piles on the side of the road and lighting them. Some people had made straw scarecrows dressed in men's clothing, which they burnt with the books. Many were yelling about how they would do the same to all terrorists and dissenters of the state.

Some of the people called to Pat and Eddy, "Have you thrown out your Bibles and books of the old-world system? You'd better because if they find them in your house, they'll arrest you!"

Others laughed and called out, "That's if we don't get you first! The state has brought in citizen's arrests, you know!"

Now very much afraid, Pat and Eddy rushed down the side lane leading to their unit. Pat entered the side gate, but Eddy stepped to the side of the road to inspect something he saw there.

A police car turned the corner. The store had notified the police and described them as a very suspicious elderly couple with incorrect identification. The car pulled up, and the police asked Eddy for his One World ID card. "Mate, it's against the law not to have the correct card. You're under arrest," said the cop, and he jumped out of his car and grabbed Eddy.

Pat opened the side gate to see what Eddy was doing. She saw the police car, and she saw them handcuff Eddy and roughly shove him in the car. She was shocked and quickly shut the gate before they saw her.

Afraid, Pat crept upstairs and peeped out of the front window. Army trucks were moving slowly down the street. Black-uniformed men, with face shields attached to their helmets, were knocking on house doors right along the street. People were showing them papers or their cell phones.

Some had none, and at gunpoint they were pushed into army trucks that moved slowly by. Then a gun went off, and Pat swung around to see another trying to run. He was killed on the spot and was left where he fell. Now terrified, she had to get out of there before they knocked on her door. She quickly crept through the side gate and dragged both their cases back to the railway station. She had to get back home. Surely, she would be safe there.

At her driveway, she stood, shocked. A new locked gate had been erected across the drive. On the gate was a big plastic government notice. In large print was the word “PROSCRIBED.” The notice declared that the government had confiscated their property.

“But, how could they?” she cried in shock. There wasn’t anyone to listen to her, yet she continued to argue her case out loud. “We’ve paid for our property, our taxes are paid, and we owe no debts.”

Pat sat on her suitcase and hunted through a big bag for her mobile. She rang Elsie, their house-sitter while they were away. When she heard the house-sitter’s voice, she spoke.

“Elsie, this is Pat. What’s happened? I’m sitting in front of a gate blocking our driveway, and I can’t get in. Where are you? Are you in the house? What is this all about? We own our home. What are they doing?” she said, now screaming.

“Sorry, they moved me out. I’m back at my house. Your church is now closed because of another outbreak of the virus. Last week the police nailed a ‘proscribed’ notice to the church door. Then do you know what I was told? The police through Zoom can locate private church services in the homes. They went to these places and arrested all the families. Your church friends have been taken to the Penrith Detention Centre, and they’re all imprisoned. Also, all their possessions were confiscated. It’s against the law to worship in any other church or homes except the state’s,” she explained.

***The police through Zoom can locate private church services in the homes. It’s against the law to worship in any other church or homes except the state’s.***

A car slowly, quietly, drove up to Pat. She looked up into the faces of police now alighting from their vehicle.

“Are you Pat Bailey?” one of them asked as they roughly grabbed her.

“Yes,” she answered.

“You are under arrest. You have been classed as a dangerous dissenter of the state.”

## Chapter 33

# Notes Lying in the Streets

Jacky rushed down Anne Street on his way to Julie and Robert's unit. He was accompanied by Jim, an elderly man from the mission, who hobbled along, trying to keep up. They turned a corner to witness people being attacked by citizens.

"Jacky, is this the so-called citizen's arrest?" Jim questioned, disgusted.

The police were dragging two elderly ladies from their home toward their wagons. A crowd of people rushed forward, screaming, "What's the matter with you people? You're the cause of all these disasters taking place. God has left us because of you lot. Just take the card. How hard is that?" They spat, and pulled the smaller of the two by her hair, and punched her. The other fell, and they started to kick her. The police stood back and watched.

When the crowd finished, the police dragged the two women into their waiting wagons while the citizens spat on them and screamed, "Troublemakers of the peace!" A child lay dead in the gutter, but the police didn't make an arrest.

Jacky and Jim walked on, noticing banknotes lying in gutters and fluttering across streets. The old man went to pick them up.

"Don't bother, Jim. They ain't no use."

"Yes, so I've been told," old Jim said. "I heard that the stock exchange hit an all-time low and closed. The New World Order is now in place." He looked around at Jacky. He thought to himself, *Jacky's just a young lad, street-raised with no education, and look what the Lord has done for him.* He continued, "Mate, we're in trouble, you and me. We haven't a card for the new system. They'll get us if they find out."

Jacky barked, "No way! I ain't following 'em, and they're not havin' me!" With his head down, he studied one of the notes.

"Jacky, most people have left the cities. Don't you have somewhere you could go?" Jim asked.

"I ain't got a home to sell, and I ain't got folks, so I'll stay 'ere to help you lot."

"Thanks, Jacky. Any rate, it's too late to leave now. It might still be time for people on small blocks to leave and move into isolation, but it's definitely too late for city folk." Jim thought for a few minutes and continued, "You know, Jacky, it reminds me of the Second World War. Only a few Jews heeded signs and left before the war started. They were given plenty of warning by Hitler. He said continually, '*Jude Rous'* — 'Jews get out.' Some waited until they could see the implications, and then, it was too late for them to leave. They tried to hide, but most were found and killed. The stubborn ones that refused to leave their expensive homes were rounded up and—well, the rest is history." He stopped and rubbed his old hips. They were really giving him heaps of pain.

Jacky nodded as he watched old Jim. He wondered how the old man was coping with all the work at Julie and Robert's unit, where the mission was secretly operating.

Jim got to the point. "Well, it's the same for these poor people whose plight we have just witnessed. They have no way out. Look up there." He pointed to the black helicopters hovering overhead. "Do you know they have satellite-linked technology up there? It's made it possible for government personnel to track people and listen to their conversations in their homes. Also, there are 5G poles everywhere taking photos of our activities, and our cell phones also allow them to track us. What hope do we have?" He looked around to see if they were being followed and then added, "In the city we're under attack. The United Nations helicopters can immobilise cars and all the traffic on the road until an arrest is made. And what hope do we have on foot?"

"Hey, ya know, I saw that!" Jacky butted in excitedly.

"Yes," responded Jim, "so did I, the other day. The choppers hovered above, and all the cars instantly stopped in the middle of the highway." Throwing his hands in the air, he continued. "They all stopped. People got out of their cars and looked up at the choppers. Some even shook their fists at them." He laughed sourly. "Then the police came on foot and on motorbikes and grabbed the people."

Jacky walked wordlessly as he thought of the people still in the city. Many were eleventh-hour Christians who came to the Lord after the New World Order came into effect. They saw the implications of the new system and stood on the side of truth and Bible principles. They never had a chance to leave, and now they had to stand firm, sealing their faith and lives with their deaths.

Jacky thought of his people and his own circumstances. *He and his people, the people of the night, were the poorest and most oppressed of all, but God had given them work to do. They were proud that God had chosen them. They were thrilled that He loved them, and with this knowledge, they weren't going to let Him down. No! Death had no sting for them; it was an honour to die for their Saviour.*

Jacky and Jim turned a corner and headed toward the unit. There were crosses painted on many letterboxes.

"COVID-19—This time, it has come back ten times worse. It has hit 'em hard," Jacky remarked. "My people have been helping."

"Is it true what they say?" Jim asked. "The affected families are forbidden to go out of their homes in case they infect others, and they pay for someone to bring food and medical supplies to their front doors?"

Jacky nodded.

A tall, very thin lad came to the gate. "Stay on the other side of the street, you two. I don't want to infect you. I have to change in the backyard shed. I've set up a little personal decontamination centre in there."

Many of Jacky's people provided this service at the doors. It gave them a chance to tell the afflicted people and their families about God's love for them, and they shared their knowledge of natural medicine while assisting at the doors. They never entered, as it was against the law. It was also a great risk to their health.

"Do you clean the clothes and cans of food they give you in that shed?" Jim nodded toward the shed.

"Yes, I wash them in a tub of disinfectant," the lad called back. "Later this evening, I'll bring around what I have at home."

Soon they were at Robert and Julie's unit. They entered the lounge room to find new people gathered there. Families with small children sat quietly on foam mattresses and ate gratefully the meal offered to them. Some hadn't eaten for many days.

Jacky's people worked quietly and respectfully. They were changed and no longer criminals of the city or people of the night. Their rags had been changed for neat, clean, second-hand clothes obtained from others for their caring acts. They were respectable and had a purpose for the first time in their lives. Their purpose was to share Jesus' love with the city's lost.

Many people attending had studied before with Jacky and were going to be baptised that evening. He prayed and then spoke to them.

"Remember, Jesus is like a mother hen. He will place His wings of protection over you. Do not be afraid."

They all went outside. In the backyard, the tank next to the shed was half-filled with water. One by one, they were baptised by full immersion. Their faces lit up, and the glory of the Lord rested upon them. God's angels drew close and watched the scene.

Helicopters, like a swarm of black bats in the evening sky, passed overhead looking for the unwary. Their radars scanning through the atmosphere for their prey, beeping quietly in their cockpits, they searched with advanced technology and equipment all the homes below.

Everyone held their breath and prayed. The choppers passed over as if the people below were invisible. God's covering was over them. They praised the Lord for this miracle and went home rejoicing.

# Chapter 34

# Penrith Detention Centre

In solitary confinement deep in the bowels of the earth at Penrith Detention Centre, Pat sat in her stone-walled prison cell and listened fearfully. Screams and cries echoed through the walls. She sat in darkness with only a crack of light shining through the hatch in her door. In the darkness she contemplated what she needed to say in court the next day. She knew God would bring to remembrance things she had studied. She prayed for wisdom and help in these matters. She thought of poor Eddy. She hoped she would see him in court. He would be worried about her.

She heard the familiar rattle of a food trolley and people's voices coming down the hall. Soon, her hatch was lifted, and a woman's face appeared. It seemed kind enough. The woman looked over her shoulder and then slipped a bag on the tray with Pat's meal. She tapped it with her finger. "Shhhh."

Pat quickly took the tray. The hatch came down, and she was back in darkness. She fumbled about the tray and found the bag. In it were a piece of paper and something long and hard—a torch. Fumbling some more, she found the switch. She turned it on and found the paper that had fallen to the floor. Picking it up, she read:

> *My name is Rose. I was in court relieving the court's stenographer when your husband went through. The words he spoke are written on this paper. When I heard him speak, I was impressed by his quiet manner. I listened to all he said, and I gave my life to God. I'm about to make my stand. Please pray for me, and if we don't meet again, we will meet in heaven on the sea of glass. Use this torch to read the walls.*
>
> *Christian regards, in Jesus' lovely name, Rose.*

* * *

Pat quickly placed the tray on her bed and beamed her torchlight on the walls. To her amazement, the walls were covered in Bible texts. "Thank You, Lord," she whispered in awe. She started to read.

By the door she found, "The earth shall be full of the knowledge of the Lord as the waters cover the sea. Isaiah 11:9." Then she read on the wall near her bed, "Come unto me, all ye that labour and are heavy laden, and I will give you rest. Matthew 11:28." Nearby was, "He that overcomes shall inherit all things: I will be his God, and he shall be my son. Revelation 21:7."

"Yes, Lord, as your child, I trust and love You," she whispered. She picked up her burger with one hand and held the torch in the other. She shone it on the wall next to her and read, "I will not leave you comfortless; I will come to you. John 14:18."

She shone the torch on the letter on her bed that held the details of Eddy's trial. She opened it anxiously, wondering how he had coped. The court case had been recorded by Rose in this fashion:

JUDGE: Are you Mr. Edward Bailey of 167 Western Ave, Hornsby?

EDWARD: Yes, Your Honour, that's correct.

JUDGE: I realise you have been a Sabbath-keeping Christian all your adult life. I have sat in this courtroom for the last few months listening to all sorts of tales. I now want to hear about your beliefs, and especially where it tells you in the Bible about your Sabbath.

EDWARD: Your Honour, it states in Genesis, "God rested on the seventh day and sanctified it." In Exodus, we learn of the Ten Commandments written on stone by God. In the fourth commandment, God explains exactly how to keep His Sabbath day. In Revelation chapter 22, verse 14, it says, "Blessed are they that keep God's commandments." From the first to the last book in the Bible, it talks about God's rest day.

JUDGE: Yes, but these laws were fulfilled at the cross.

EDWARD: Yes, fulfilled but not finished. The ceremonial laws were completed at the cross. They were written by man. God's laws written by Him will never change.

JUDGE: Yes, I see your point. But in this court, your beliefs are acts of treason. Court dismissed.

* * *

The next morning, the warden escorted Pat to the local courthouse. She waited in a spacious reception room with many other dissenters. People sat, stood, and leaned against walls. The accused were of all ages, and she noticed many were young people. All seemed perfectly calm.

A man stepped out from one of the many courtrooms. "Mrs. Pat Bailey. Mrs. Bailey, please come with me."

Pat followed him into the courtroom. Inside a reporter took her picture. News reporters were allowed to follow the procedures in court. The authorities hoped it would put off others from following this despised group of troublemakers. Of late, however, it seemed to have become fashionable to become one of them. People by the millions across the world had stepped out and followed this minority group.

They took Pat to her seat. The stenographer entered and sat ready. The judge entered, and all rose. A man stepped forward and held a heavy Bible in front of Pat. She pledged she would tell the truth and only the truth, and then she was told to sit.

The female judge spoke. "You are Mrs. Pat Bailey, of 167 Western Avenue, Hornsby. Is that correct?"

"Yes, Your Honour."

"I believe you refused to swear allegiance to the One World Government and its church. Is that correct?" The judge now looked over her glasses.

"No, just the church, Your Honour. I keep the Sabbath of the Bible, God's day, and the government church doesn't."

"Well, that may be the case, but this isn't a religious court hearing, but a civil matter. The people have voted for Sunday across the world, and the international courts of the United Nations have agreed. You do realize you will be forbidden to buy and sell, and you will be held in prison as a terrorist if you don't sign these papers in front of you. I'm sure it's a misunderstanding, and you will sign," the judge snapped.

Pat quickly read the section about the new church. "Your Honour," she said, "it says that I must agree to follow its laws and keep Sunday as the day of worship."

"Yes! That's correct. It's for the good of mankind. All past wars have been religious wars, which we can't afford at this time in history. It will bring world peace, and after all, you're still worshipping the same God, so what's your problem?"

"Your Honour, Sunday isn't God's day of worship. The Bible says ..."

"Mrs. Bailey, it's not a religious debate. I can see you are very stubborn, and for this, you will have to pay the price. Case closed." She banged down her hammer, closed Pat's files, and left the room.

Pat, out of frustration, hung her head and cried. She had been sentenced guilty without a trial. She was led out through the court's back door.

# Chapter 35

# Prison

Pat sat cross-legged on her bed with her torch in hand, examining her walls. She praised God daily for the scripture written there. She was so busy that she didn't even hear the noise of the food trolley. Suddenly, the hatch rattled, and light flowed in, and Rose's face peeped in at her. She stood and walked to the door. Rose handed her a tray.

There was a note under her food:

*Pat, I am going to leave the city today. I believe it's hard to get past the chopper patrol, but I have my One World ID. Please pray for me.*

*Christian regards, Rose*

*P.S. Eddy is in a cell across from you. I managed several days ago to smuggle in an old watch for him. He passed me a note today. He said to tell you that he will tap on the metal surround of his hatch with his torch; one tap for Sunday and two for Monday, and so on. He will do this at 8 pm when the guards have gone home.*

*How wonderful,* Pat thought. *Now I'll know the time and day. I am so glad to hear Eddy is alive. I'm going to miss Rose and her little notes, though.* "Please keep her safe, Lord," she prayed. Pat didn't realise that Rose had shared the same news about Eddy to all the other dissenters in the nearby cells.

Pat stood by her hatch. It must be getting close to 8:00 p.m., she thought. She listened for Eddy's tap. Yes, there it was, one—Sunday, two—Monday, three—Tuesday, four—Wednesday, five—Thursday, six—Friday. Friday night, the beginning of the Sabbath. She stood for a moment or two, still listening. Was that singing? Yes, muffled voices were singing a hymn. She joined in. The voices became louder and louder and sweeter and sweeter. It was beautiful. It sounded like a choir outside her cell, in the courtyard above.

Pat sat on her bed and sang as loudly as she could. She realised she was singing with heavenly angels that came to comfort the inmates on their Sabbath. Tears soaked her face as joy filled her heart. *If this is what heaven was going to be like, how wonderful it will be,* she thought.

She sang on, and so did her cellmates. The prisoners in other cell blocks, who were there for terrorism or theft, listened in wonder. *Where was this choir coming from? What glorious singing,* they thought.

* * *

In the morning, male voices echoed down the corridor. Pat's door was opened, and she was shoved with others into the bright morning light. She stood in the sudden light, half-blinded and trying to focus. Yes, she was in the courtyard. What was that across the yard? Was she seeing correctly? It looked like a row of old-fashioned guillotines. Surely not! Fear clutched her heart, and she felt violently sick. Where was her resolve, her faith, her strength now? Panicking, she looked for Eddy. He was standing beside her, silent and grey. She grabbed his hand while he stood staring ahead.

A group from another block of cells was led out, and the people were placed behind each guillotine. Eddy gasped and whispered to her, "That man on the end—that's the judge who asked me about my faith! I wonder if he made a stand for Christ. He was very interested and didn't disagree with me."

They watched the judge closely. He seemed perfectly peaceful. The other prisoners walked like zombies. They tripped and could hardly stand, and their eyes were glazed; they were obviously drugged.

The people's heads were placed in a harness, and their necks stretched over the blocks. There were no ropes to pull up the guillotines; it was an electrical system with one operator.

Some of the condemned sobbed or begged, but peace surrounded the judge. He raised his eyes to heaven. His face shone as if God was showing him heavenly scenes.

In unison the blades came down with a sickening thud. A groan rose from the onlookers, who held their heads down, eyes shut. This shocking scene they wished not to witness. Many vomited on their way back to their cells, and most sobbed; some fainted.

Time went on, but there wasn't another mass execution. The cries of inmates being tortured stopped. Eddy and Pat wondered what was happening and sat in their dark cells, waiting.

## Chapter 36

# The Pope in Jerusalem

In Jerusalem Pope Nicholas and his representatives from the ten world zones sat with the United Nations Israeli General in his private office. The Israeli General was explaining the procedures implemented to prevent war in Israel. He said, "The United Nations Defence Force has recruited the world's best brains and capabilities in warfare. We have satellite and laser techniques, and instruments of warfare advanced beyond those possessed by any nation of the world. We have kept this information a secret for such a time as this. In the Mediterranean Sea, we have battleships with navy helicopters stationed aboard, on high alert to protect the boundaries of Israel. We have increased the United Nations' army in Jerusalem. Soldiers with the latest technology of warfare are stationed along the city wall."

He spoke about the Islamic children. "They are taught to chant slogans against people who disagree with their nation's beliefs. They are taught hostility from the cradle and how to get even with people of the world. They talk openly to world reporters about America being an evil nation."

He shrugged. "But we're not too worried. Their hate will change when they are rejected by nations of the world. We have plenty of oil, and if necessary, we can do without them. They will be starved into submission if they don't accept the new system. Meanwhile, we will bring radicals on the borders to order. The Sunnis and Shiites must realise the importance of working together for peace."

The Israeli General finished his speech, and then Pope Nicholas stood. "On the subject of peace, plans have been made for peace with the Muslims of the world. If they accept the New World system, we will make their beliefs an important part of the One World Church. This will make them key players in the scheme of things. They will also be honoured and rewarded in trade and commerce by the United Nations World Council. We will give them recognition above all other nations; that's what they have sought after for centuries. Doing this, we expect the wound of rejection to be healed, and we will then have peace with this nation; but they must abide by the United Nations and its Church to receive these privileges. The United Nations president is calling for a meeting next week to discuss these plans."

The meeting broke for thirty minutes. Steven and Brad, on guard duty, quietly discussed all they had heard.

"I hate to think what's going to happen when the nations hold the Islamic people so high in the One World Government," Stephen mused. "You can't undo centuries of brainwashing and conditioning to hate as easily as they think. It might work for a short time, but then they'll want full control of the world."

***You can't undo centuries of brainwashing and conditioning to hate as easily as they think.***

"I remember reading about Islam being raised in the Dark Ages to fight and destroy the Jews and early Sabbath-keeping Christians. They were to capture Jerusalem for the pope. They did this, but when the powerful generals of the Islamic armies were to surrender their power, they refused, and wouldn't give Jerusalem to the pope. Do you think anything's changed?" Brad asked.

After the break, the Head of Antiquities in Jerusalem stood and discussed the diggings. Maps were projected onto a wall. "The ark vanished when Jerusalem was under siege. Babylonians destroyed the temple, but they didn't take the ark," he explained. "If it wasn't taken to Babylon, it was most likely hidden."

He pointed at the map behind him. "We needed a clear guideline where to dig. We gathered the best minds on this subject, and this is what they came up with.

"When the Babylonians attacked, it would have been impossible to take the ark outside the wall without the soldiers seizing it." He looked around, pleased with himself, and jabbed at an area just outside the wall of Old Jerusalem. "The people would have travelled through Hezekiah's tunnel to reach this area."

A film replaced the maps, showing a passage deep in the quarries. "In order to reach the secret passage, we sent a thin young man down to crawl for many metres through this narrow tunnel. It was about a metre in height. A short while later, the young man found himself in a larger passage. He was at the extremity of the quarries at this point and moving under Jerusalem in the direction of the Temple Mount. Suddenly, he came up against an ancient, fortified wall and had to come back. We will work with an archaeologist to find the best way to penetrate this wall," he explained. "The whole place is strewn with rubble and honeycombed with old walls and hollows from many ancient buildings. We don't want to bring the whole city down on our heads." He laughed heartily at his own joke.

They all joined in and laughed and clapped, and then the meeting was closed. They went to a banquet held next to the seminar room. All relaxed, and as they ate, they discussed further events.

* * *

Several days later, the thin young man stood at the designated tunnel again. "Here, lad, strap this hand drill and these rods to your back. This will leave your hands free and make it easier for you to crawl through the tunnel. Try not to stir the dust, or you'll choke," laughed the tough, careless guard.

The lad crawled and, in places, wriggled on his stomach. Eventually, he slithered into the larger tunnel at the wall and was able to stand and drill. He sent buckets of sandstone dust on a rope to the opening. The sandstone wall was thick and nearly impossible to penetrate.

The guard outside stood and stretched. It was hot, and he was getting impatient. "Boy," he said roughly to a small boy who had been working all day, pulling at the rope retrieving buckets of stone dust from the cave. He grabbed the boy's shoulder, and the boy winced, as his muscles were sore and the guard's hand hard and cruel. "Boy, you've been working for hours. What's happening?"

At that moment, a call went up from the youth in the cavern. "I've got through! I'm shining my light through the hole! I've drilled through the wall!" His yell was muffled by the narrow tunnel and the thick dust. There was silence as all waited for more news.

Scraping was followed by billowing dust, as arms, then a head, wriggled out amongst clouds of white stone dust. The lad coughed and choked. All waited as he washed out his mouth and drank away the dust in his throat.

"I've found the treasure," he coughed. "There were lots of things lying about the floor and a large box in the corner. They all looked like the drawings you showed me."

Everyone stared. Then a loud cheer echoed around the hills. To the amazement of all, the youth had found Solomon's treasures. The stone box probably housed the ark of the covenant.

Great excitement came over the men as they studied their maps. They discussed the position of the treasure and decided on a plan of action: they would enter another tunnel on the opposite side of the ancient quarry.

# Chapter 37

# Selected Tunnel

The next day, the group travelled down a tunnel on the other side of the quarry chosen for its width; the previous tunnel was too narrow to bring out the treasure. They travelled for some time and came to another fortified wall.

"Step back," whispered one of the officials, and he pulled his comrade back. "If it's the right cavern, the contents might have special powers."

Once again, they used drills and rods on the ancient sandstone wall. Many hours later, they peered through the drilled hole and—presto—they were looking into the artifacts chamber, the chamber they were seeking—and so far, they were all unharmed.

That evening, they sat around a table and discussed plans to enter the chamber. First, they had to contact the pope and Jerusalem's governor. All were very excited and could hardly wait, but all knew this was a deadly secret they couldn't share with anyone.

* * *

In the meantime, in another area of Jerusalem, an important event was taking place. A long line of cars drove through magnificent gardens and parked in designated areas. World rulers and officials alighted amidst peacocks, rare exotic birds, man-made waterfalls, trees, and bushes from all over the world. They walked slowly through the park staring in amazement. The official buildings and gardens that had risen from countless hours of convict labour were now officially complete.

The delegates passed the partly-built replica of Solomon's sandstone temple with its large brass pillars. It was simple but startling. They wondered if the ark had been found.

They then drove to another part of the city and entered the Vatican's Cathedral that had been built many years before. Brad and Steven once more stood on guard duty. The dignitaries entered and marvelled at the great treasures brought from the Vatican before they were shown to their seats.

Pope Nicholas entered, followed by a choir. They were the worlds' best, selected from Catholic churches worldwide. As they sang, the acoustics, which had been a vital element in the cathedral design, amplified the breathtaking music, taking all to another realm. Everybody's senses were captivated, and all came under the spell of their surroundings.

Pope Nicholas prayed and conducted High Mass. When completed, dignitaries entered a vestry under the protection of Brad and Steven. Here they sat, and food and wine were offered while the pope spoke to them.

"The United Nations has met with the Islamic representatives, and peaceful negotiations have taken place. They have signed an agreement to adhere to all the regulations required of them. *Peace and safety* have been assured by all for our world," said Pope Nicholas, smiling broadly. "Let us raise our glasses in a toast."

They all raised their glasses in unison and cheered, "World peace and safety!"

Pope Nicholas waved them back to their seats. "My main place of residence will be at the Vatican, but I will regularly visit Jerusalem as this is where the One World Church headquarters will be situated.

"At our conference we appointed a new cardinal for Jerusalem. You are well aware of this, as most of you were present. The cardinal chosen needed the skills to keep Christians, Jews, and Muslims at peace. We have great pleasure in introducing you to our new cardinal for this region," he said with much pomp and grandeur.

Cardinal Christi entered. This was the first time all those present met this stranger. He had a majestic countenance and was tall, young, and extremely striking. Islamic by birth, he had been brought up in his early years in Israel as a Jew, educated in England in his teens in a Catholic college, then transferred to the Vatican in Rome to complete his training for this post. Who was this man? Nobody really knew. He had been orphaned at birth and had lived with many different families, so the story went—how did he get to such a high position in Rome?

The meeting over, Brad and Steven returned to their room. Steven voiced his thoughts. "Our Christian-Jewish friends have been very concerned about staying in this city. They feel it's time to head for the hills. I think I'll go with them."

"I'm with you, mate," Brad said.

* * *

All through the Middle East, people saw visions of Mary. Countless people testified to seeing her—above mosques and churches, in the sky, even at railway stations. She appeared to people of all faiths and gave the same message to all: "You must abide by our New World Order. The world needs peace to survive. All mankind must work together for peace. Love one another and work together. The world needs restoring, and so does man." Her voice was soft and sweet. She pleaded for mankind. Muslims, Jews, and Christians fell to the ground and crossed themselves, calling out in praise and submission. All were afraid.

* * *

Pope Nicholas and Cardinal Christi flew back to the Vatican. They had business to complete in preparation for the commencement of the cardinal's position in Jerusalem.

Late that evening, the pope rang a bell on his bedside locker. "Christi, help me, please," he gasped in terrible pain. "Phone my doctor. Get him to come to my room. I think I'm having a heart attack," he whispered between gasps.

Many tests were conducted, and a mild heart attack was diagnosed. The doctor suggested that with rest and care, the pope's condition would improve. Cardinal Christi stayed close, attending to his every need.

The next morning, the cardinal knocked quietly on the pope's bedroom door. "Enter," said a crisp but weak voice. Cardinal Christi entered and bowed slightly to the thin figure sitting in a large reclining chair by the open French windows.

"Come over here, Christi, and sit with me for a while. I wish to discuss the procedures you need to follow at the American Congress."

Christi poured a glass of water for the feeble pope and sat down in a chair next to him. They both silently looked across the pope's private courtyard with its pretty flowering garden that attracted sparrows, which sprightly hopped around chairs and a table. It was a hot, dry day, and tree branches hung over the courtyard fence, shading a small fish pond in a corner.

"As you know," Pope Nicholas confided, "the Muslim people across the world have amalgamated their church with ours. They are now one with Catholicism." The pope nodded to Christi as he spoke. "When we meet with the One World Council next month, we must remember that we have the most members and the largest voice in the assembly. You must meet with our cardinals and make sure they understand this and explain to them that they must stand united at all times."

## Chapter 38

# Remand Centre

Meanwhile, at the Wilcannia Remand Centre, the continuous throbbing of a pump in the shallow creek indicated prisoners were at work. A call went up, and all prisoners placed their tools on the ground. They were not made to carry them back to camp as the tools could easily become weapons. The young workers marched to the road, clanging and dragging the chain that linked them at the ankles.

When they were well away from their tools, the group formed a line on the road. Several guards collected the tools and placed them in a pickup truck. Another turned off the pump.

The prisoners shambled along the road, with armed guards accompanying them. The sun beat on their exhausted bodies. They were dehydrated but were not permitted to drink while they worked. They marched, or more accurately, dragged themselves and their chains back to their compound.

***The prisoners shambled along the road, with armed guards accompanying them. They marched, or more accurately, dragged themselves and their chains back to their compound.***

As they passed the main gates, one of the young prisoners collapsed. Everyone stumbled to a halt. One of the guards yelled at a young girl who had just drawn water from the creek and had stopped to watch the men return from their labours.

"Get over here with your bucket!" yelled the guard.

The girl ran to the boy lying on the ground. "Tommy!" she whispered. As she struggled with the heavy bucket, he raised his head. "Anita, serve my table tonight. I have a message I need to give you. Be very careful not to be caught."

That evening, Anita did a swap with her friend Sue so she could serve Tommy. It meant she would be on kitchen duty, cleaning dishes, for many hours that evening, but she had to get to Tommy and receive his message.

*It must be very important*, she thought to herself, *or he wouldn't risk being shot like he did this afternoon.*

That evening in the dining hall, Anita moved slowly, dragging a heavy trolley filled with trays of food. She stopped next to an armed guard leaning against the wall. She slid a tray off the trolley and took it to Tommy. As she did so, Tommy slipped her a note. She fumbled it into her apron pocket and quickly moved to another person. All evening, while she worked, the note rested in her pocket, and she wondered about its message.

When Tommy was placed back in his cell, he could hear weeping. He turned to the guard who was locking his door. "Who's in the next cell? He doesn't sound very old."

The guard sniffed. "A troublemaker, they say. He's only sixteen, but he wouldn't recant and give up his family's faith. He kept sharing his faith. He broke the law deliberately, so tonight, they're going to make an example of him. He'll be shot." The guard grinned. "And you lot will have the pleasure of watching."

When the guard had gone, Tommy went to the wall and pressed his ear against it. "Can you hear me?" he asked. "If you can, come to the wall and place both hands on it, and I'll do the same. We can pray together."

After a few moments, Tommy asked the young fellow, "Can you hear me? Are you ready?"

"Yes, but I'm afraid of dying," sobbed the boy.

"What's your name?"

"My name is Nathaniel, but they call me Nat."

"Say this, Nat. 'Lord, give unto your servant that peace which the world cannot give.'"

Nat followed. "Lord, give unto your servant that peace which the world cannot give."

"I will pray for you," said Tommy. "Dear heavenly Father, in Your Son Jesus' sweet name, we pray. Be with Nat in these last moments of his life. Give him the sweet peace only You can give. He's about to be shot, but let him feel no pain. Let him hold on to the promise that death is like sleep that seems only a moment, and then he will meet You face to face at Your second coming, on that great resurrection day. Please, dear Jesus, we pray now for Your peace and thank You for it. Amen."

For the next hour, Tommy and Nat stood with their ears to the wall and talked of heaven and prayed back and forth. God's Spirit came into the boy and gave him peace. He was perfectly calm when guards came to take him to his execution.

Everyone was pushed into rough lines in the courtyard at midnight. Anita stood at the back of the group. Like everyone else, her heart pounded in sorrow, waiting in fear for the young boy who was to be executed.

She took out Tommy's note and read it under the outside spotlight. The note said that guards were organising to enter the girls' barracks. They intended to come sometime after midnight, to rape them at gunpoint. Anita crumpled the note in her sweaty fingers. She had to escape. Tommy had suggested that she creep to the north fence where it crossed over the creek. She was to dive deep and swim under a gap in the fence.

Anita looked around for the other girls in her barracks but couldn't see them. She had no time to find them. She didn't know what to do.

Three guards with rifles entered and prepared for the execution. A guard placed a cloth around the boy's eyes and tied his hands behind him. Youth witnessing the scene started to sing:

*Abide with me; fast falls the eventide;*
*The darkness deepens; Lord, with me abide!*
*When other helpers fail and comforts flee,*
*Help of the helpless, O abide with me.*

God's Spirit was there, and some of the hardened guards were moved to tears.

While all eyes were on the blindfolded boy, Anita quickly slipped from the light into shadows and moved quietly, carefully, down to the creek's edge. She looked to see if anybody was watching, but only Tommy watched her go.

She waded into the creek. It was shallow enough for her to stand. She walked forward to the fence, then leaned over and felt down, down, until she found the hole in the fence. She was completely submerged. She pushed herself through the hole but struggled to get through; she was stuck. She wriggled, but something held her back. She realised it was her shirt. It had caught on the fence wire. "Oh! No, Lord, don't let me die like this," she prayed.

Hands pulled at her shirt—somebody else's hands. She came to the surface on the other side, breathless and gasping. It was Tommy's hands that freed her. As they climbed the bank of the Darling River that was now a creek, they heard the rifles being discharged as the guards executed what they called "justice."

With saddened hearts, they heard singing and now screaming and crying from the other prisoners. They turned and ran for their lives and their freedom.

## Chapter 39

# A Ride That Saves Their Lives

They struggled through bushes for about an hour and eventually came to a highway. Already they were missed: they could hear prison guards shouting and dogs barking as they smelled their tracks. It was a full moon, and on the highway edge, they would be easily spotted. They stood, wondering what to do when a road train turned the corner.

Tommy jumped into the middle of the road and waved at the approaching truck. The driver pulled over several metres farther on. They ran to the truck and jumped in, hoping the driver wouldn't guess where they had come from. Luckily, the remand centre didn't have uniforms for their inmates.

They looked at each other and smiled in relief and gratitude for the ride: a ride that saved their lives. All dissenters trying to escape faced the firing squad, just as Nat had that very evening. They both said a silent prayer of gratitude to their heavenly Father.

"I'm heading down to Hay. I'll pull up there for breakfast and a rest," said the driver. "Where are you two going?"

"Sydney," Tommy answered.

"Well, I'm going to Melbourne. You'll need to catch another ride at Hay. You need to get onto the Mid-western Highway and catch a lift to Bathurst."

"Thanks, we will," Tommy said.

For the rest of the journey, the driver talked to a woman on his two-way. He was more interested in flirting and talking nonsense than asking the two escapees questions. This suited them, and soon both were sound asleep.

They were woken much later by the driver, who shook them. "Come on, you two, I have to go."

They yawned and opened their eyes to see beside the truck another person with their driver. Tommy sat bolt upright. Did the driver report them? Who was this other bloke?

"Here," said their driver. "I've bought you both a bottle of Coke and a packet of chips. I dare say you're hungry." He fished around in the sleeping quarters of his cab and produced a backpack. "Use this to carry the food," he said, placing the goods in the bag and handing it to Tommy. "This here's a mate of mine. You'd better go with him; he's going in the direction of Sydney." He stepped aside and let the kids out.

Soon, they were travelling to Bathurst with their new truck driver. His rig was much smaller than his friend's. This driver was very talkative. "There are more and more 'proscribed' notices on property gates," he said. "They say the owners are traitors to the state because they won't join the New World Order. I don't blame them. I can't see how that could trouble the state. I don't believe in the new system, but I go along with it so I can earn a living."

Tommy and Anita watched as farms passed by. They were shocked by the number of houses, sheds, and land that had been burned out by bushfires. Millions of hectares had been destroyed in New South Wales and rural Victoria from fires caused by heatwaves and electrical storms. Tommy realised planet-warming conditions and the lack of rain had caused devastation everywhere. Conditions on the planet were out of control.

"See! See over there on the gate," the driver continued. "It's a 'proscribed' sign. Those people will be in the lockup at the moment. If you're hungry, go to their homes. There'll be gardens, more than likely, that you can help yourselves to. You might even find a bed."

They pulled up on the side of the road. Their trip with this talkative chap was over. "Oh! By the way, kids, keep to dirt tracks if you don't want to be picked up," he said without a smile as he pulled out and drove away.

"I think he knew. Actually, I think they both knew. No wonder. Look at us. We're filthy, and our clothes are torn and muddy," Anita said, dismayed.

"I'm glad we drove with him. He's told us so much. The cities are filled with disease, people rioting, and others killing terrorists and dissenters. I don't know if we should travel back to Sydney," Tommy said.

Anita's situation with her parents came sharply back to her. She still found it hard to believe. She realised for the first time that she had no one to go home to. She felt very frightened and alone.

They walked down a dirt road, taking the driver's advice. They were tired and hungry and not sure what to do. They were on the run. They were villains, escaped prisoners, because they loved the Lord and His commandments. Well, they would continue to pray and rely on Him.

Soon they came to a gate with a "proscribed" sign. The notice, like all the others, said the farm had been confiscated.

"Let's go up and see if they have a garden. We might be able to get into the house and have a nice shower," said Anita hopefully.

When behind the house, they noticed a dry creek bed with only mud puddles. Next to its bank was a small home garden. They picked what wasn't wilted and placed the small offering in Tommy's bag. They tried the trees and managed a few lemons. The fruit on the other trees had dropped, as had their leaves, from the drought conditions.

At the house, they looked in windows and tried opening doors. Suddenly, a shot was fired. A man ran toward them, waving his shotgun and shouting and swearing.

"Run, Anita, to the road, and if you can, get a lift away from here," Tommy shouted as he ran out in the open and led the man away from Anita.

"But where will I meet you?" she yelled.

"Just go, Anita—go now!"

She ran down the drive onto the dirt road. Suddenly, a car pulled up. A lady leaned over and opened the passenger door. "Get in quickly before that hopeless Jack Brown sees you and reports you to the police," said the stranger.

Anita dutifully climbed in, surprised at the stranger's words. She stared at the lady with questions crowding her mind.

"That old Jack Brown dobbed in his neighbours, the Lewis family, for not going along with the state laws, and now he takes to anybody who comes on their property. He has a vendetta against everybody, especially terrorists and dissenters of the state." She looked around to gauge Anita's response and continued. "I go around and rescue you strays, regardless of why you're on the road, before he can cause trouble."

She took Anita to her home. After a nice warm shower and dinner, Anita relaxed in the lounge room, wearing her new friend Lynn's pyjamas.

Lynn continued her story. "There's a reason why I do this. My daughter refused to join the One World Government and its church. She joined an underground group while she lived and worked in Sydney. She's in prison now for going against the government. You know, she never had a chance to explain her faith to me. I would love to know more about it," she sighed.

"Well, I can tell you," Anita answered. "Do you have a Bible?"

## Chapter 40

# Tommy Outruns the Farmer

Tommy had outrun the farmer easily. He now followed a disused railway track fifty meters from the highway. It ran in the same direction as the road but hidden by bushes and trees. Kangaroos bounded across nearby paddocks, and wild goats chewed on saltbushes dotted here and there. Stars hung bright in the cool evening sky, and an occasional bird call broke the silence. He was glad the moon gave plenty of light as he followed the railway line.

Tommy had walked half the night when he came to an abandoned railway station. Peering in, he noticed the stationmaster's room had an old bed in the corner. Squinting into the dark corners of the room, he checked for unwanted snakes or rats and mice, which he didn't want for company. Dragging the bed toward the doorway, he checked under the blanket for other pests. Sinking gladly onto it, he dropped into an exhausted sleep.

Suddenly, from nowhere, came the roar of engines and yells of voices. Local hooligans were on a night hunt, their spotlight beaming into the stationmaster's room. Guns fired, and bullets showered into the bundle of blankets on the bed. Shouts and laughter followed. They were on a man-hunt, and it was great sport for them. As quickly as they came, they went.

Tommy wasn't there. He was watching from a disused railway carriage. In the middle of the night, a dream had woken him. He had seen the very scene that had just taken place. He had risen and stumbled in his tiredness across a paddock to a wagon and squatted in the corner as the roar of the four-wheel-drive came closer and closer. Faint with fear, he watched the hooligans fire into the little room. He was grateful that he had acted on his dream; getting up and moving had saved his life. He sent prayers of thanks for his deliverance.

***Tommy wasn't there. He was watching from a disused railway carriage. In the middle of the night, a dream had woken him.***

Even though they had gone away, he had to get out of there quickly. *They might come back and find me,* he thought.

Once again, following the railway track, he prayed to his heavenly Father, thanking Him for sparing his life.

It was early morning, and the day promised a heatwave. An hour later, Tommy found himself facing another unexpected problem in the shape of two fierce dogs that ran at him from the gate of a nearby garden. They were Australian Kelpies. He picked up a stout stick to defend himself.

He was fighting a losing battle when a large man appeared carrying a gun. The man was brawny, with a long beard and matted dreadlocks. One word from him sent the dogs scurrying, but by then, Tommy's legs and his right ankle had been badly torn and were bleeding.

"Those dogs are vicious! You should keep them locked up! They might have killed me!" Tommy shouted.

"That's the idea," growled the man. "I'm sick of you city people coming and stealing our food. There is a depression, you know, and the only food we have is what we grow." He jerked his gun toward the middle of a dry paddock, and Tommy could see a crumpled figure on the ground.

"What's the matter with him?" he asked.

"Nothing now, because he's dead," the man snarled.

"You shot him? But why?" Tommy said, reeling back in horror.

"I'm not letting any of you near my family; you may have the virus. I believe it is breaking out again. Get going; if I have to kill you, so be it." He waved his gun. "Get on your way, and don't come back this way begging. I and my family intend to stay alive. This farm isn't a charity. Do you hear me?" he roared. "If you come back again, the bullet will be for you! Now get going while you still can!"

Tommy ran and was soon on another narrow dirt road. It looked more like a war zone, with bodies sprawled in gutters and across the road. There were others in a nearby paddock. He quickly slipped into bushes and ran toward the highway. He was in shock and couldn't focus on the enormity of the horror around him.

Once on the highway, Tommy walked slowly out of exhaustion and despair. A motorhome drove quietly alongside him. He looked up into Julie's and Robert's faces. *At last—friends! Thank You, Lord.*

Tommy climbed into the bus, and someone threw herself at him. It was Anita. They hugged and cried together.

Anita told him her story. "A lady picked me up last night. Her name was Lynn. She took me back to her farm. That evening, we studied late into the night, and Lynn gave her life to Jesus. I tried to get her to come with me, but she feels she must help stranded people. When morning came, Lynn drove me along the highway to look for you, Tommy. We came across this motorhome—it was Julie and Robert, and they found you just after they found me," she said, grinning widely.

"We're taking you both back to Shangri-La," laughed Robert as they headed up the highway.

# Chapter 41

# Diggings

Digging continued in Jerusalem. The fortified wall was broken down, and the engineers placed large, heavy steel reinforcement beams at its opening.

The Department of Antiquity's archaeologist and the secretary-general of the United Nations entered through its opening with bated breath and hearts racing from excitement and anticipation. With stone dust thick in the air, they stood amongst the lost treasure of Solomon's temple scattered about the floor.

The head of Antiquities was a Jewish archaeologist who was well aware of all objects that belonged to the temple.

"It looks as if someone was in a great hurry when they placed the treasures here. These most important artifacts are scattered everywhere," he muttered as he looked around. "Yes!" he exclaimed as he pointed from the opening. "That's the altar of incense—and look across the other side of the room—the altar of burnt offerings!"

He looked at the others with a face radiant with anticipation and joy. "Oh! The box over there, I believe, houses the ark. This is modern history's greatest find," he said, grinning. "So far, so good. Now, what to do? It's very unsafe to enter, and especially to open the box. I think we should withdraw and hold council." He ushered his companions out of the tunnel, leaving guards at the cave entrance.

They met with the leaders of Jerusalem and the United Nations secretary-general. "We have two youth employed here as secret CIA guards. I've been told on good authority these men are part of a new underground group. They are dissenters who refuse to join the global government and its church. I've kept them under my nose so I could perhaps catch others here in Israel. Let's use them to open this box, and if it's the ark, they can remove it to the museum, ready for when Solomon's temple is completed. We'll see how powerful their God is," he said, sneering.

Brad and Steven were called to his office. Their orders were given. That evening, under armed guard, they were to remove artifacts—and specifically the ark. They were dismissed and went to the kitchen for their midday meal, where they sat in a corner quietly considering their new orders. Brad was very much afraid. He was a new Christian and didn't understand the covenant story. "Will we be killed if we move those things?" he whispered.

"Don't worry," Steven whispered back. "When Jesus died on the cross, God's glory departed from the temple. This was indicated by a heavy veil being torn from top to bottom by invisible hands. It was an end to ceremonial sacrifices. Jesus had fulfilled the service as God's Lamb by dying on the cross for you and me. We will be under no threat when we handle these things. But if God's presence is still there, I believe with all my heart He will protect us. Let's not tell them. They might leave us alone for a bit longer. This might be our chance to escape," he added.

"Fancy them knowing all along about us. I feel we're in big trouble," answered Brad.

"We're told in these last days it will be the same for churches as it was in Old Jerusalem. You know. I was told that the ark will be brought forth from its hiding place. When we see this, we will know the time of the end is here," Steven explained.

"Yes, and like Old Jerusalem we are surrounded by a real army. You know, we must escape now before Pope Nicholas and Cardinal Christi return," Brad said, very agitated.

The evening was cold and bleak. COVID-19 was raising its head once again in Jerusalem. It was early March, with unusual storms and gales. Three official army trucks stopped at Jerusalem's heavily guarded gates. Brad and Steven sat in the first two trucks. The third carried soldiers.

Brad and the driver were in full uniform. At the gates, Brad flashed his United Nations identification card while families hid under blankets in the back. They sat with hearts thumping so hard it made it hard for them to breathe. "Please, God, make sure a child or baby doesn't speak or cry and don't let them inspect the truck." Brad prayed silently.

As his vehicle passed through the gates, weather conditions caused interference with satellite surveillance equipment. The next truck, with Steven in front, had the same success. "Thank You, Lord, for your covering and help," Steven prayed.

They were about half a kilometre down the highway when an awful explosion was heard, and red-hot flames flared in their rear-vision mirrors. When the third truck with army personnel, who were on an unsolicited agenda, passed the gates, the surveillance equipment had come back in focus, and the truck exploded, and all were killed.

Brad placed his finger on his lips to indicate complete silence. He motioned with his hand for the driver to move, move, move, now.

The heavy rain and sleet made it difficult for them to move quickly. Brad looked up for choppers. The weather was too rough for them to be a threat. God was certainly looking after them.

Several hours later, both trucks turned off the highway and stopped on a secondary road leading to a small fishing village. Brad and Steve pulled back the flaps of the trucks and helped out the women and children sitting wide-eyed and frightened inside. In little family groups, the passengers clambered down and straggled toward the village.

Brad and Steven watched them out of sight, then reversed their trucks onto the highway and drove them to a petrol station, parking next to a toilet block where they changed into black coats, trousers, and woollen beanies. They had a few supplies and a change of clothes in their backpacks, plus a sleeping bag.

They walked quickly back along the road. The night was black, and they hoped and prayed they wouldn't run into pursuing vehicles. Soon, they were at the village and boarding a fishing vessel with the other families.

Their boat slipped silently from the fishing ramp. As they travelled out to sea, Brad and Steven stood on the deck, watching police check parked cars and people boarding Haifa's ferry. Originally, they had planned to use this ferry themselves, but at the last minute, God gave them a strong impression to go another way. Arrangements had been made to travel on this fishing vessel to the island's city, Nicosia. They gave grateful thanks to those who helped them and to their Lord for His protection.

# Chapter 42

# The White House—America

Cardinal Christi flew to the White House in America for the world's first "United Summit Meeting," with the ambassadors of the United Nations and the New World Government. Each sat with mask and had appropriate distance between seats. A loud and energetic debate took place among all the different government leaders. After a long and drawn-out discussion, a vote was taken. They all voted in one accord for a universal death decree. It was to be executed in fourteen days' time. All countries across the globe would be notified. All must strike on the same night a decisive blow that would utterly silence the voice of dissent and reproof against the New World Order for once and for all.

Cardinal Christi travelled to England and selected twelve good young community-aware men as his personal aides. Their heritage was Islamic, but they had been educated in the Western society as he was. They would travel and assist him on his world mission for peace.

***All must strike on the same night a decisive blow that would utterly silence the voice of dissent and reproof against the New World Order for once and for all.***

First, they visited the Islamic people and received their approval and blessing, and discussed the Vatican's promises to them as a nation. They then travelled to the main capital cities of Europe, where people were mostly Catholic. These people followed their beloved pope then, and now, without question. Cardinal Christi and his twelve disciples stood in front of huge crowds of converts. They cried out, "Cardinal Christi represents our Holy Father, Pope Nicholas."

Next, they travelled to America, where famous preachers hosted a national program to introduce Cardinal Christi. It was to have world coverage. The Crystal Palace in California was chosen. It was a massive church, but that evening it was more than filled to capacity. People outside watched on large TV screens. The young didn't care about health rules and crowded together.

To keep the crowd entertained before the meeting started, young, energetic singers filled the stage. They wore jeans and casual tops. They sang and danced to the famous Rock Demons, the nation's top rock band. The crowd stood and sang and swayed to the music. Some wore masks but most didn't.

The building was filled with youth from all walks of life. The sick and lame sat near the front. Many adults sat at the back where the music wasn't so loud. So all could see, TV screens were placed throughout the massive church.

When all were seated and quiet, Billy Jones, the famous charismatic preacher, entered the stage. "Brothers and sisters of the world, I wish to introduce Cardinal Christi."

All stood, clapping and cheering, as Christi and his disciples entered the stage. He stood quietly, waiting. He and his disciples wore simple white gowns. Christi's dark hair was tied in a ponytail. His beard was soft and short. His appearance was ordinary, but somehow his bearing made him majestic. His dark eyes, gentle but wise and knowing, held all.

The cheering crowd became quiet. They stood in awe. His stillness and strength brought peace to all present. He indicated for them to sit. He raised his hands and spoke in a clear, strong, yet subdued voice.

"I'm here to represent God. He's my Father, and I wish all humankind to know His love and peace. He told me to bring this peace to you. We must join together in God's love. As the representative of God, the Catholic Church has the power to change His Word. The One World Church is God's power on earth, and we must all work together regardless of our past creeds and doctrines. God wishes you to have His peace. Now let us pray."

Cardinal Christi and his disciples then slipped quietly away. What seemed a spiritual spectacle followed, as ghostly images floated over and around the congregation. They said they were spirits from the dead and spoke to their relatives attending the meeting. Many healings followed.

Mary appeared, brighter and larger than the rest. She spoke to all in the congregation. People of the world watched, amazed, and cameras zoomed in on her serene and beautiful face. This was certainly the grand movement to bring in world peace.

# Chapter 43

# Death Decree

Evening came, and the stone tablets from Jerusalem were unveiled. The unveiling was beamed across the world through a Christian satellite TV station. Reporters were invited to attend. God's people in isolated, unknown places watched where possible. A supernatural shaft of light shone on the stone, directly over the fourth commandment. God showed the world that the Sabbath was His ordained day.

The phone rang at the Vatican the next morning. Pope Nicholas answered. He was told about the unveiling of the stone tablets. "Who gave permission for these artifacts to be transported to America?" he screamed.

People across the world heard stories of these artifacts that displayed God's commandments. It was in Hebrew, but a translator was brought in, and the world saw for the first time the exact words God wrote about His Sabbath day and how they were to worship on that day. They went back to their ministers and asked about these truths. They were told it wasn't important as it was a Jewish law done away with at the cross.

Pope Nicholas organised a meeting in New York with the United Nations and world church leaders. He was still very weak, but he knew if he didn't do this quickly, his plans would fail. Many wore masks and were appropriately distancing from each other.

Without a mask, the pope stood in front of the world leaders. "Leaders of the One World Government and its church, I wish to talk to you. The churches of the world have voted and agreed on a Sunday rest day. This is to give the planet rest from pollution and rest for the families of the world. People across the world are from many cultures and beliefs, but they have joined together for peace and prosperity and trade benefits. To keep peace, we must all agree with these new laws. We must focus on the new order if we want to receive God's blessing and world peace. To oppose this program will bring God's wrath upon the earth. God is not worried about the day as long as we worship Him and work together in peace," he explained carefully. "Now, I must encourage you, leaders of the world, to enforce the universal death decree, which has been passed by you."

* * *

The people were certainly deceived. Men believed in the last great delusion because they believed in man and his lies. The only way they could distinguish between error and truth was through the Holy Scriptures, which they had forsaken.

* * *

Across the world, Jews, Christians, and Muslims gathered at the Rock in Jerusalem. All believed that Jesus was returning to usher in one thousand years of peace. Throngs of people gathered and waited with great expectation and excitement for His appearance and His instructions.

Suddenly, in unison, the throng shouted and pointed. "Look! Christ has returned! Look! He's coming with all His angels!" they shouted and prostrated themselves in fear and dedication. All about them was a brilliant light, and angels with Jesus and his twelve disciples were seen. They didn't realise they were deceived. Evil angels were depicting Christ's return. In the brilliant, glowing light, "Jesus" with his mother Mary and his disciples stood side by side and could be seen by all.

He stood in front of the terrified people and spoke in a soft voice. "This is the beginning of earth's Jubilee and its one thousand years of peace. All countries of the world have united in peace and prosperity. You must do all I command," he explained.

* * *

God's people knew better. They knew from scripture that Jesus would return with countless angels and not touch the earth. They knew the dead were in their graves and couldn't speak, and Satan would present a counterfeit that resembled the true. God's people knew they were only to follow the Word of God. They weren't to follow man's traditions. Not one "jot or tittle" should change from the law until all was fulfilled.

# Chapter 44

# Bondi Beach

In the middle of the night, deep in the ocean above New Zealand, two massive ocean plates—or ocean floors—ground together. They moved, and the sea bed exploded.

High in a luxury apartment at Sydney's Bondi Beach, George Smiggs, a visiting business executive, stepped out onto the balcony. His mind was filled with business problems that made it impossible for him to sleep. He stared at the flat, quiet ocean in the full moon.

Suddenly, a rumble was heard in the distance as a massive earthquake erupted. A loud, hissing, sucking sound, rather like the noise of a jet engine, came from the ocean. The ocean pulled back, and back, and back farther.

George stared at the receding water. He knew this was how tsunamis started. The ocean went back a very long way and then came in at enormous speed.

He wasn't going to be caught. He grabbed his car keys and trousers, which he struggled to climb into as he ran downstairs, and jumped into his car. He drove as fast as he could, all the while watching the distant ocean behind him. He turned the corner and headed to the Western Highway. Many others were doing the same. The road became congested as people tried to flee from the disaster heading their way. Confusion broke out as others joined the escape. Soon, the highway was completely blocked. George abandoned his car and followed the panting, pushing people as they ran from their useless cars in the direction of the foothills, many kilometres away.

There were screams, horns blasting, people cursing and swearing. People aroused by the noise came out of their houses and stared.

Suddenly, there was silence—an eerie silence that made all stop and look and listen. Then suddenly, a heavy rumbling shook the ground under their feet.

George looked around, and there it was, a giant tsunami wave consuming all in its raging black wall as it moved forward in the grey moonlight.

It crashed through high-rise buildings, crushing them like a pack of cards, bringing debris and objects toward him. Soon it towered above him and crashed over him and all who stood staring into its bowels.

It came once, twice, three times. One wave rolled closely behind another, each larger and higher than the one before, each destroying more and more in its path.

The next morning, Australia's east coast was a ruin. From Wollongong to Brisbane, all was destroyed for many kilometres inland. The cities and towns looked like war zones. Millions upon millions were killed, and millions more remained homeless. The cities, already devastated with disease, now had countless bodies lying flung amongst ruined buildings. The heat brought flies, flies that swarmed and crawled over dead bodies.

United Nations' black helicopters filled the sky. They swooped down on the devastated cities and towns in ruins. They sprayed the coast extensively with their burning yellow gas to hold in check the diseases that now threatened in the scorching summer heat.

There was devastation and more devastation everywhere. A massive global relief effort took place, but millions remained homeless.

Australia's already-fragile economy completely toppled.

## Chapter 45

# Chemical Weapons

Jacky rushed down Bridge Street, away from the slums of Sydney. As he ran, he looked at the unfortunates who lay dying in alleyways and in the doorways of houses of ill-repute. He saw trucks parked ahead and drivers carrying out the dead in body bags. They threw them into the backs of the trucks. He knew they would take the corpses to tips, where they were buried in mass graves.

Disease had taken over the city. It reminded Jacky of the Black Death stories from Europe many centuries ago. It also reminded him of the mass graves in Hitler's days.

Evacuation had been organised for the inner city, with all shops closed and the people leaving for country retreats.

The cities on the eastern coast of Australia looked like war zones with destruction and devastation everywhere. Only the poor still remained and those without correct identification. The helicopters patrolling the streets now blocked those without One World identification cards from entering and leaving the cities.

Jacky watched government drones fly overhead. They dropped a chemical weapon in the form of yellow gas over buildings, cleansing them of all rodents and germs. It also killed those who refused to move from their hiding holes and alleyways. He watched to see the direction in which the drones flew. He didn't want to be caught by their poisonous gases.

The drones had digital surveillance that recorded people running to churches and crowding the already-full vestibules. Most now lay within doors, dying terrible deaths.

Jacky ran in the opposite direction. He had organised ambulances to pick up officials from Sydney's Government House. They were very ill with the virus and were to be transported to Springwood's convent. Jacky was anxious to travel with the ambulance. He wanted to see Sister Maria and hear her news. This was the only way he could pass the city's boundary guards. He knew that walking people, unidentified, had no hope.

* * *

That evening, at St Mary's, he lay in a convent bed. A full moon shone, and there was barely a sound to be heard. He listened closely and soon heard a possum or two scampering across the roof and a tree branch softly swishing across his window. It was so, so different from the city with all its crime, disease, and death that brought such sadness. He lay and thought of Sister Maria and what she had shared with him. He was thrilled to hear that Father Frank had given his life to the Lord before he died.

# Chapter 46

# Blue Mountains

A few days later, Jacky stood at St Mary's Convent gates, waiting for Sister Maria. They were going to escape into dense bush—who would know where.

Sister Maria and Jacky stumbled through the night. They had found a narrow track, and in the moonlight, they carefully clambered down the mountain. Soon, the sun rose over the tops of tall gum trees. The *wheeeeee-ep* crack of whipbirds sounded close by in the crisp mountain air. The chortle of a kookaburra and its mate's answering cackle could be heard. Then, in the distance, they caught the sound of singing.

As they approached the valley, deep in the Blue Mountains behind Sydney, they saw people sitting by a river. A small waterfall with clean, pure water cascaded over a rock face that framed a large cave.

Sister Maria and Jacky hid in the lantana and watched and listened. A man sat on a rock, strumming his guitar as people sang. Beautiful voices behind and beside them joined the singers. Jacky and Sister Maria swung around to see who was nearby. There was nobody to be seen, but the voices were very close. They seemed right next to them.

Jacky's eyes boggled in fear. Sister Maria placed her finger on her lips. They lay and listened. The voices sang hymns of praise in beautiful unison. The singing that surrounded them was sweet and pure. It was heavenly.

Sister Maria whispered, "We're in the presence of heavenly angels. The angels have left the non-praying, faithless people and joined God's people."

***The voices sang hymns of praise in beautiful unison. The singing that surrounded them was sweet and pure. It was heavenly.***

Jacky nodded.

They watched the people below gather something from the trees and ground, placing it into bowls. They looked up and noticed small white petals fluttering from the sky. *Maybe they're falling from flowers in the trees*, thought Sister Maria. Some fell in the lantana bushes, which were prickly and bare because of the drought. The smell of honey was thick in the air.

Sister Maria held out a hand and caught some petals. Up close, they were small, crisp flakes, smelling of honey. She tasted them gingerly and grinned widely. "Come and eat, Jacky. It's heavenly manna, like in the Bible!" she practically shouted.

The people below looked up, hearing her voice. Sister Maria and Jacky scrambled down to them. It was their friends, Julie and Robert and their family, and Tommy and Anita, and others. Hugging and rejoicing, they were relieved to find each other still alive.

Sister Maria and Jacky shared their news about the devastation happening on the coast of Australia and across the world.

"That's why we've been left alone!" exclaimed Julie, looking at the others. She and the others had been safe at Shangri-La and didn't realise what was taking place upon the earth. She explained to Sister Maria and Jacky, "Before, the choppers passed overhead all the time. We thought they were scanning for unidentified persons like us, but they always went away, and nothing happened."

Robert broke in. "We wondered why we hadn't seen the choppers for some time. Now we know." He smiled sadly.

Julie continued with her story. "Some time ago, we were woken by shouting and crying. The cries were heart-wrenching. We traced them to caravans and tents.

"'My babies are dead!' a young woman told us. Another person said, 'All the old folk are dead! They died in their sleep!'

"All here at the camp wondered what was happening, and they came to us for answers."

Robert spoke again. "We told them we must be nearing the time of the plagues, and God has put the young, old, and sick to sleep out of kindness. This was some weeks ago," he repeated.

* * *

The days quickly passed for all at the retreat, but, of course, there wasn't any news. They had to live by faith and spent their days in prayer, but Satan still tried to torment their minds. He impressed upon them that they were without hope and that God didn't love them. Satan kept telling them to go back to civilisation. But they stood steadfast and kept praying.

## Chapter 47

# Planet Warming

Reporters across the world interviewed a leading scientist at the National Science Institute. "Today, we see the results of the United Nations' lack of serious commitment toward dealing with planet changes. Since in power, they have given more attention to politics than to scientific reports. They were told to quickly change the world's use of pollutants, but too little, too late, has been achieved.

"Ten years ago, we argued with them for change. Back then, the temperature had risen one degree, and we saw small glaciers in the Andes disappear. We saw major changes to China's population from this small weather change.

"Over the past ten years, the temperature has continued to increase. Last year, the global temperature increased up to four degrees, and we saw a decrease in water availability across the world. Small islands vanished as ocean levels rose. The rising water levels created havoc in Florida. New York is having destructive winds with flooding. London's Thames River floodgates are now compromised, causing massive flooding in London. Millions of people in Africa have starved, and millions more are suffering from a huge increase in malaria. We begged the United Nations to enforce drastic measures. They started a few programs, but as I have already said: too little, too late.

"We are now experiencing the result of a devastated planet. It has come many years earlier than even what we predicted!" He thumped his hand on the desk in frustration as he fought tears of despair.

The viewers witnessed hurricanes and tornados hitting Central America. A roving crew of TV reporters in America's central farming area came on air. "We are seeing devastation never before recorded." A cow spun through the air in a tornado, narrowly missing the film crew's camera. "Look, did you see that?" the announcer screamed, and he turned and looked behind. "There are cars and even buses being caught up in the tornado. They're being tossed through the sky—and look over to the right. Just look at that! See, in all that junk flying about? It's a plane. Yes, a plane is falling from the sky!"

He screamed, buffeted by the wind. His film crew shot him staggering, and then there was static, and then nothing. They went off the air.

A reporter in a studio came on air. “Tsunamis have hit America’s southwestern coast. Japan and most of Australia’s eastern coast have also been devastated by tsunamis. The countries’ coastal areas are in ruins. Ships across the world have been lost in turbulent oceans,” he announced. “We are recording a meltdown of the icecap at the North Pole. The ice is crumbling into the sea at incredible speed.”

As the world watched and witnessed these devastations, panic overtook multitudes, and terrible scenes followed.

People across the world staged mass riots in the towns, hamlets, and cities. Civil war broke out in the city of New York and many major cities of the world. Men, women, and children marched with hand weapons of whatever shape or size they could find to the United Nations’ buildings. They screamed and waved their arms in protest and fury. In hostility they turned on other protesters in their way. They plundered shops and destroyed cars and buildings. Their anger and noise were explosive. All hope was lost. All were maddened with despair.

The confederacy of evil joined the confederacy of men. Satan’s evil angels came down upon the earth in force. They encouraged and entered men with evil instructions, and men became insane with bloodshed and violence. They maimed and killed all in their way. They scrambled over dead bodies lying in the streets. Their screams joined the screams of demons, sounding across the sky as they whipped earth’s elements into chaos.

***The confederacy of evil joined the confederacy of men. Satan’s evil angels came down upon the earth in force. They encouraged and entered men with evil instructions, and men became insane with bloodshed and violence.***

The United Nations’ armies prepared for civil war, and men’s hearts shrank in fear. Through the smoke and mayhem, black helicopters covered the sky. Men in black protective clothing, with helmets shielding their faces, slid down ropes from choppers hovering above. They hit the ground running and firing special laser guns.

Protesters screamed and withered on the ground in great pain as the soldiers attacked. Blood ran in the streets from the dead and dying.

It was impossible to restore law and order from that moment on in New York and all the capital cities of the world. People witnessed the events on their TVs.

Max Hiller was interviewing an American scientist. Dr. Hanson spoke in a tightly-controlled voice that sounded nervous. "I have been asked by NASA to warn the people of the world of a disruptive, catastrophic event. In the last few days, we have been watching global devastation as never before because of planet warming. We have watched the great meltdown at the North Pole. We have watched tsunamis destroy cities around the globe. Now, another catastrophe is about to happen.

"In the middle of the nebula of Orion is a brilliant light; scientists at NASA believe it is a comet travelling toward earth. Because of its brilliance, they speculate that it is a comet of great size and heat. Even if it doesn't hit us, it will certainly upset the earth's electromagnetic field. We have never experienced such a phenomenon as this in the past. We will update you further as we get more details."

"Tell us about the earth's electromagnetic fields," urged Max Hiller.

"The earth is a huge magnet," explained Dr. Hanson. "Through climate change, with the planet warming, the atmosphere on earth has become a lot hotter. When the core of the earth becomes disturbed through planetary changes, the magnetic field around the earth also becomes disturbed. When this happens, we are in real trouble." He lowered his voice, which noticeably shook. "Doomsday type of trouble."

"Some people say that if this happens, the poles will shift. Do you think the comet will upset the earth's magnetic field and cause its poles to shift, and will we have another ice age?" squawked Max Hiller, his normally suave voice high-pitched with fear.

"We don't know what's going to happen. I wish to make no more comments on the subject," answered Dr. Hanson.

# Chapter 48

# Penrith Remand Centre

At Penrith Remand Centre, people lay in their cells, moaning as they died. Their stomachs contracted in pain, and they rolled into a fetal position. They were dying of thirst. Each had been given a small bottle of water some days ago, but many days had now passed, and they had been forgotten by their wardens and left to die.

Once-able men screamed and banged their empty metal food containers against stone walls in the hope of arousing someone—anyone at all—but there wasn't anybody to hear their cries or even care. All had gone and left them in captivity without their daily needs.

Pat and Eddy and their dissenter friends were in a separate area of the detention centre. Pat heard a faint tinkling sound and looked toward her food hutch. It was lifted by unseen hands. A bright light shone outside in the passage. A plate with food that looked like wafers and smelled like honey was placed on the ledge, along with a bottle of water.

Pat knew her ministering angel was taking care of her, but she felt low in spirit, even though she knew God was protecting her. If she could have seen the other dimension, she would have realised her cell was filled with evil angels. As they pressed down on her, they whispered to her mind that she wasn't saved, that her sins weren't forgiven.

"Oh, please save me, Lord Jesus," she sobbed. "I know You love me, and I know that I'm protected by your angels. Please take this deep depression from me."

As she pleaded with God, heavenly angels came down and dispersed the evil angels. For a while, Pat looked into heaven with her face lit up, and then evil angels once again tormented her soul.

It was the same in other cells where those classed as dissenters for God were trapped. These pale, weary saints continued to plead their case before the Lord. Tired and isolated, they didn't know that their probation had closed. They were God's first fruit. Their case had been decided in heaven. Unknown to them, Jesus had taken off His priestly robes and placed on His kingly robes. He had left the court of heaven and was preparing to take them home.

* * *

In courtrooms across the world, discussions were taking place about the impending death decree. In one Australian courtroom, a government official spoke. "A law was passed by the United Nations. Today the world is making ready to enforce this law. All nations of the globe must strike a decisive blow tomorrow at midnight. Let's get organised and make arrangements to implement the death decree tomorrow in our prisons." He turned to the Australian United Nations Police Force. "You realise," he sneered, "this law will rid the whole world of troublemakers, once and for all."

At midnight, the time of the scheduled execution, a terrible storm broke, with thunder, wind, and rain. The wardens had returned to their detention centres. As they entered, they covered their noses. The stink of dead bodies was intense.

"Joe, did you check on those religious nuts?" one of the wardens yelled.

"I did, and they're all alive, and by the look of them, in good health. Impossible bunch to get rid of," he answered.

"Well, Joe, don't worry. We'll get rid of them tonight, once and for all," answered the warden. "We must prepare for the execution. Even though we have this freak storm, we have to get the courtyard ready. After the execution, they'll bring in trucks to cart away all the bodies."

A rumble was heard, louder than the thunder roaring overhead. "What the heck?" Joe screamed. A huge explosion shook the detention centre. The walls in each cell in the dissenters' quarters were smashed to the ground. A large angel stood in front of each opening, ready to escort the praying ones to safety. The prisoners ran quickly into the courtyard.

Eddy ran across the courtyard to Pat, who stood perfectly still. "Quick, let's get out of here," he said breathlessly. Pat, numb with fear, couldn't think or speak. Eddy grabbed her hand and dragged her along. "Come on, Pat. Let's go."

Prison guards ran with guns pointed at them. "Stop, or we'll shoot!" they shouted. They raised their guns to fire, but the mighty angels of God, now visible, held up their hands, and the guns fell like straw to the ground. The wardens covered their faces and stumbled backward in fear.

# Chapter 49

# NASA Observatory

At the NASA observatory in America, scientists sat at satellite-linked computers and watched the comet come closer and closer.

"Neil, are you seeing what I'm seeing? My monitor is linked to earth's electromagnetic responses and is indicating that the earth's surface is starting to break down."

"Yes!" yelled Neil. "I can see it!"

"What's causing it?" a junior scientist asked.

"It's the planet's electromagnetic field," answered Neil, "and look—it's happening across Europe and here in America. The approaching comet has brought this on. We must ring the White House and warn the president."

He picked up his phone, but before he could call, a huge earth tremor rocked the floor under them. Some people fell over, and others grabbed their desks. Neil watched on his computer as the forces of inertia reacted to the shift of matter.

"Look!" screamed one of the other scientists. "The oceans and lakes have jerked in a different direction. Look—the earth's crust has broken open in Mexico and South America—and across the equator! My monitor is mapping volcanic eruptions in these areas." He held his hands over his face and moaned deeply with the thought of the devastation taking place outside the observatory. Others grabbed their phones to check with loved ones and make arrangements for their safety.

Neil scanned his computer. "We're having a major overflow of lava, which our monitors indicate will flow into waterways and eventually, the oceans."

Before he could continue, his phone rang. It was the president of the United States. "Yes, sir, that is correct …"

People everywhere felt the huge tremors and stood waiting in fear. Nuclear power stations across the world leaked radiation upon the people in their vicinities, adding more death and poison to the atmosphere.

Fire engines, police, ambulances, and emergency vehicles wailed past horrified communities, racing to areas of devastation.

Swiftly, paramedics and hospital staff, dressed in dark protective uniforms and masks, entered affected areas. When finished, they went through a series of procedures in emergency decontamination chambers. These had been hurriedly set up in the ever-growing number of emergency tent hospitals across the nation.

# Chapter 50

# Fireballs

Now, the trumpets of Revelation began to fall. Heaven was lit with balls of fire that had arrows darting out of them. They struck the cities of the world. Not all at the same time. They seemed to be raining down from the same spot in heaven, and as the earth rotated, other cities were struck, and great calamities followed.

The first city in America to be struck was Nashville. Here stood the replica of the original Parthenon of Athens. The building was plain but had pillars around its porches. Inside was a forty-two-foot statue of Athena dressed in gold. It represented the sun god and sun worship. God was not pleased.

Following was New York and Capitol Hill, plus all the high buildings gracing this city.

Jerusalem, with its new temple-museum and sanctuary service of old, was the first in the Middle East to meet its doom.

Across the world, large mansions and businesses were set on fire, and no human effort could extinguish the flames. The earth quaked, and homes of the rich and wealthy were crashing down. There was confusion everywhere. People were screaming, and demons were screeching. People were praying prayers that were now too late.

Other cities also met their fate. All were struck by these great balls of flames with shooting arrows.

The wrath of God was raining down on the people of the world.

* * *

The United Nations quickly called a meeting with the ten nations of the world.

A delegate spoke. "The Vatican has let us down. They encouraged us to instigate a 'Socialist World System,' and who has benefited? Them, of course. They said God will honour us by enforcing the people to go back to church and keep Sunday as a family day of rest and worship. They told us we must care for the planet and the community, as this was the only way the planet would survive. The pope sat in our meetings and said if we put these measures in place, God will heal the planet and restore order. Look what's happened. God is angry with us. The Vatican only cares about power and rulership. They have deceived us."

* * *

In the middle of the night, three black jets flashed across Italy's sky. They were above for a moment or two and then out of sight, leaving their supersonic noise trailing in their wake. These United Nations superfast Tomcat fighter planes were on a world mission for peace. Where they came from and where they were going was top secret.

At a great height, they now passed over the city of Rome. Through special satellite screens, they could see high-rise buildings, once lit like Christmas trees, now some partly lit, but most in ruins and darkness. This was caused by the great devastation now taking place on the planet. They saw night traffic trailing in a thin line that looked like glittering diamonds strung on a fine track of black metal. Once, they would have jostled each other on congested highways. Highways that shone with brilliant lights were now mostly in black, velvety darkness.

Italy's armed forces were below, concentrating on protecting the Vatican City that miraculously was still intact. They had placed tanks and machinery of warfare around its perimeter.

The men above knew all this would soon disappear. As they approached their target, the Vatican City of Rome, they signalled to each other. "Mission! Destruct! Hit target now! Over and out!" called the lead jet.

Warhead nuclear missiles shot through the earth's atmosphere. As quickly as they came, they went. Their jets disappeared in the darkness of the night.

People of Rome looked up and saw great shafts of fire spearheading down over the Vatican. All stood and stared, wondering what they saw. It was a spectacle of fireworks of a different type. It would mean the end of the Vatican and all its treasures and wealth—the Vatican, whose bank made world merchants rich, the Vatican, whose pope was head of the One World Church.

A terrible explosion with nuclear fire followed. All was lost, and the Vatican completely destroyed. The explosion shook Italy and nearby countries.

The world watched and wept ... for the loss of their wealth and the loss of all hope, as the Vatican and Rome burned.

The United Nations had turned on the Vatican. She now received the same fate the rest of the world received.

* * *

In heaven Jesus stood and ceased His intercession in the heavenly sanctuary above. He lifted His hands and, with a loud voice, declared, "It is done. Every case has been decided for life or death. Probation for the world has closed."

At this time, there were only two classes of people in the world: those who were loyal to God and those who stood under the banner of the Prince of darkness.

***Another warlord stood on a mountain ridge in front of his men. It was Lucifer, once the great archangel of heaven, now aged and grotesque through centuries of evil.***

Max Hiller sombrely shook his head in disbelief as he announced, "A painful, severe, weeping sore is spreading on the people's bodies. In many places across the world, life in the sea is dying, and rivers and springs have become impure. Dead plankton has made the waters thick and red like blood. It's like the blood of a dead man," he screamed, his voice growing hysterical. "It seems many cities have only blood to drink. Yes, it seems that's all they have."

He stopped and calmed himself before continuing. "There's no clean water in many cities. Desperate measures need to be taken to purchase water somewhere, somehow," he added in a low, despairing voice. "The ozone layer is completely destroyed, and the sun is scorching us. It's burning like searing fire. The World Health Organisation has ordered all people to stay indoors until further notice."

* * *

Another warlord stood on a mountain ridge in front of his men. It was Lucifer, once the great archangel of heaven, now aged and grotesque through centuries of evil. Once, a beautiful angel of light who ministered in the courts of heaven now looked like a menacing, black hawk balancing on the edge of a mountaintop, an evil thing of darkness about to prepare his armies. These armies of countless legions of evil angels stood before him, prepared for battle.

These evil angels knew Christ was passing through space and would take His subjects from them. They were preparing to fight Christ and His angels. This would be the great battle of Armageddon that originally started in heaven.

## Chapter 51

# Huge Hailstones

God's people rushed up mountains as hailstones, like huge blocks of ice, destroyed all in their path. The few buildings that were left standing were smashed like straw. Cars left unattended on roads were crushed into the asphalt and the earth heaved in these elements of destruction. Screams could be heard from the pursuing wicked. "Get behind these rocks!" screamed some. Others hid in mountain caves. "Curse God and all His dread followers!" another screamed. Their shouts and blaspheming of God could be heard over the roaring elements. They screamed in fear. They screamed in anger. They screamed for the mountains to protect them and repented not.

Pat and Eddy reunited with their friends, Robert, Julie, and their children, plus Tommy, Anita, Jacky, and Sister Maria, and many others. They were unharmed and were glad to see each other, but couldn't stop to talk.

Heads down, they scrambled up the mountain. They stepped over a fallen barbed-wire fence and hurried up a mountain track. At the top, they looked to the east. Their faces, lately pale, anxious, and haggard, now glowed with wonder.

Thunder and lightning roared across the sky. In the thunder God pronounced the hour of His coming, and they all cried out in joy. The wicked only heard the elements' terrible roar and trembled in fear. It was midnight, but the geological polar shift caused the aurora's brilliant moving light to shine like day.

The shift of the magnetic poles caused great earthquakes that shook cities and villages, which lay in heaps. The mountains had moved out of their places and left large caverns. The sea had thrown out ragged rocks, and more rocks were torn out of the earth itself and scattered over the surface. Huge trees were uprooted and tossed over the land.

Soon they could see with their naked eyes a black ball in the sky, about the size of a man's fist. Jacky pointed. "Look! Christ is coming to save us!" The same cry went up across the world from God's people.

The aurora shimmered with beautiful colours and suddenly became brilliant as countless angels from heaven filled the sky. In the brilliant light, the Son of God could be seen. All around the world, man witnessed Jesus' second coming.

He raised His arm and called to the dead in Christ. They rose from their graves, and the living joined them in the air.

Great men, mighty men, and all those who chose to follow the world, perished in their hidden dens and mountain tops.

Jesus spoke, and His voice was like many instruments. "My faithful children, you stayed true to Me under great persecution. I have come to take you home."

As He spoke, His faithful followers disappeared in misty clouds in the brilliant aurora light that surrounded the earth.

Then commenced the Jubilee, with the earth void of all human life, for one thousand years.

# Epilogue

This story is a PARABLE of the last days on planet earth. This is the author's perception of the world's final events, but in reality, what is about to come upon us is greater than one can anticipate.

- Many of the miracles written in this story have already happened at a different time or place, and to different people. Some have been predicted to happen.
- World control by secret societies is fact.
- The accounts of terrorist actions have been taken from news reports, and the details changed for the purpose of publication.
- Planet warming is documented from news reports. Names and places have been changed for the purpose of publication.
- Corona virus is documented fact. Scientists are now predicating that in the near future it will mutate from person to person in plague proportions.
- The stone caves below Jerusalem are visited regularly by tourists and Freemason groups.
- The Jewish people reclaimed their land in 1967. This is the beginning of the time of the last generation.
- The pope signed a treaty in 1993 to regain Jerusalem's Temple Mount.
- It is a fact that the papacy has many buildings and churches in Jerusalem.
- It has been said the ark of the covenant has been found in the caves below Jerusalem, but not yet brought to the surface because of unrest in the area.
- The Jewish people are discussing a return to sacrificial services right now in Jerusalem.
- The Bible talks about the three angels' message.
- Revelation talks about the plagues as written in this story.

*Luke 21:32: "Verily I say unto you, this generation shall not pass away, until all be fulfilled."*

ARE YOU THIS GENERATION?

We invite you to view the complete
selection of titles we publish at:
**www.TEACHServices.com**

We encourage you to write us
with your thoughts about this,
or any other book we publish at:
**info@TEACHServices.com**

TEACH Services' titles may be purchased in
bulk quantities for educational, fund-raising,
business, or promotional use.
**bulksales@TEACHServices.com**

Finally, if you are interested in seeing
your own book in print, please contact us at:
**publishing@TEACHServices.com**

We are happy to review your manuscript at no charge.

www.ingramcontent.com/pod-product-compliance
Lightning Source LLC
LaVergne TN
LVHW050645100826
845148LV00011B/1981

* 9 7 8 1 4 7 9 6 1 3 9 3 9 *